A Kind of Justice

An anthology of mystery, suspense and horror

Judith R. Parker

Hard Shell Word Factory

For Adrianne Lee and Jo Dereske.
Two of my favorite authors and two wonderful women.

ISBN: 0-7599-0334-4
Trade Paperback
Published February 2003
© 2003 Judith R. Parker

Hard Shell Word Factory
PO Box 161
Amherst Jct. WI 54407
books@hardshell.com
http://www.hardshell.com
Cover art © Dirk A. Wolf
All rights reserved.

All characters in this book have no existence outside the imagination of the author, and have no relation whatever to anyone bearing the same name or names. These characters are not even distantly inspired by any individual known or unknown to the author, and all incidents are pure invention.

Table of Contents

Gossip	4
Eyes	18
See Skeeter Run	26
Escape	40
Bug Off	44
The Dark Fuzzies	53
The Revenge of Henry Montrose	63
Blind Justice	69
Trick or Treat	75
Threadneedle on the Loose	81

Gossip

SIMON THREADNEEDLE stared down at the body oblivious to the activity around him. The old woman was crumpled on the floor beside the overturned wheelchair, the back of her head smashed like a ripe cantaloupe. The skirt of her brown cotton dress ruched up to display pathetically swollen knees and grotesquely deformed ankles.

He knelt and pulled the skirt down. He picked one of her hands and studied it. The hand was thin, almost skeletal but the nails had been shaped and buffed. His glance traveled over her dress. It was old and beginning to fade, but clean and carefully mended. His gaze settled on the torn threads at the throat. He bent for a closer look. Old pin holes were clearly visible above the tear.

From behind him, one of the tech boys said, "Sarge, the Medical Examiner's boys are ready to take her away."

"Yeah."

Threadneedle stood up and moved away, scrutinizing the room. Like the woman, it had a neat, scrubbed look despite its obvious age and the vandalism.

Vandalism. The word made him pause. He studied the pile of books on the floor, then the cheap, painted bookcase. The books hadn't been searched. Someone had simply tipped the bookcase over, then straightened it. His gaze swept the room again. The daybed had been stripped, drawers dumped out of the bureau. Not searched, just dumped.

He squatted down and began to sort through the piles. The articles of clothing were few, mostly worn but were clean and had been neatly mended. Under the clothes, he found a few papers, mostly rent and utilities receipts. Near the bottom of the heap was a bank savings book showing a balance of one hundred thirty two dollars and sixty-seven cents accumulated over the years by monthly deposits ranging from five to ten dollars. The only other interesting items were a large box of envelopes, three pads of inexpensive stationary, a roll of stamps, an address book and a brochure from an investment firm.

Threadneedle carried the address book to the couch, sat down and began to leaf through it. It contained eleven names and addresses. All but four had been lined out and various dates ranging over the last ten years neatly written across the lines. He pocketed the book, then prowled around the room again. His attention settled on the overturned wheelchair and the black and white afghan crumpled beneath it. The afghan caught in the wheel lock lever as he righted the chair revealing an empty brown leather binocular case. He searched the room again until he was sure he hadn't overlooked the binoculars.

Jason Stone turned from packing up his fingerprint kit as Threadneedle moved into the tiny kitchen and asked, "You through in here?"

"It's all yours, Sarge."

Only the residue of fingerprint powder marred the immaculate counter top. He opened a cabinet and frowned at the three cans of pork and beans, a can of tuna and a can of Spam that were carefully aligned on the otherwise empty shelves. He moved to the other cabinet. An open box of crackers, four tea bags, part of a box of corn meal and a can of baking powder were neatly arranged. He closed the door and opened the refrigerator. A hunk of surplus cheese, a tub of margarine and an open can of condensed milk sat in lonely splendor.

He pulled open the vegetable crisper and his interest quickened. Behind a used tea bag wrapped in foil and a dab of tuna in a container, he spotted the head of lettuce. He pulled it out. Plastic. He emptied the contents onto the counter.

Della Wakefield's little hoard of treasures winked up at him. A silver pin set with turquoise and pearls, an old fashioned wide gold wedding band, a dainty engagement ring with a single diamond of perhaps a quarter carat weight and a 1917 penny. He put them back in their hiding place and returned the fake lettuce to the refrigerator.

Leaving the kitchen, he made a quick survey of the equally tiny bathroom and found nothing of interest. The big front room was empty when he returned. He stood staring thoughtfully out the big bay window. There were no trees, no birds within sight of the window. What had Wakefield watched through the missing glasses? Across the street, the whole block was lined with three and four story buildings. Shops, ranging from an oriental grocery to a pornographic bookstore, occupied the street level. There appeared to be a variety of offices on second floor of several of the buildings, and the rest seemed to be apartments. He watched a young woman in one apartment, clad only in bikini panties, doing exercises.

He turned as the door opened and his partner, Brian Cully, strode in. "What have we got, Simon? Another dope-head looking to support his habit?"

"Not this time."

Cully looked around the room. "That's what it looks like to me. An old lady living alone. Easy pickings. Probably thought she had her life savings stuffed in a sock someplace. Tore the place apart looking for it."

Threadneedle shook his head. "Look in the kitchen. She didn't have money enough to eat. Must have taken her whole income just to keep a roof over her head." He began to stroke his lantern jaw with a stubby finger.

Cully's shoulders straightened out of their usual slouch and his interest quickened. He'd seen that mannerism before. He waited for Threadneedle to tell him what was on his mind.

Simon dropped his hand and said, "This place wasn't searched but somebody wants us to think it was. Let's go talk to the neighbors."

Back at the station, Cully hefted a meaty hip onto the edge of the desk as Threadneedle settled himself in his chair and began to stroke his jaw.

"You're doing it again, Simon."

Threadneedle raised a bushy eyebrow.

"For Pete's sake, you heard the neighbors. She was so crippled with arthritis she almost never went out. Shopping once a month. Never had any visitors."

"Oh, yes, she had visitors."

"An old man once a month and the young woman two or three times a year."

Threadneedle pulled out the address book and thumbed through it. He listed the names and addresses on a sheet of paper, making a check mark by those that had been crossed out. He wrote a separate list and handed it to Cully. "Check out the

Rev. Thomas Beldan and Elizabeth Moore. I'll take the other two. We'll worry about those that were crossed out later."

When Cully was gone, Threadneedle dialed the number of Marcia Sonnenburg in El Centro. As he waited for the call to go through, he wondered where the hell El Centro was, from the area code he guessed it was some little town out in the desert. He let the number ring a dozen times before giving up and headed out to interview the last name in the book.

The address listed was an office building on the verge running down. Alvin Weiman turned out to be Dr. Weiman. There were half a dozen elderly people in the waiting room and beside the receptionist's window a hand letter sign proclaimed that Medicare and Medicaid Payments were accepted.

Threadneedle flashed his badge and a few minutes later was escorted into the doctor's office. He barely had time to seat himself in the one chair not piled with medical journals before a harassed-looking young man charged into the room, tossed several files on the all ready cluttered desk and fell into the swivel chair. "Police? So, what do you want?"

Threadneedle's eyebrows rose. "You're Dr. Weiman?" He didn't look old enough to be out of high school, let alone medical school.

Weiman was obviously used to this reaction, for he grimaced and said, "I assure you, I'm a licensed physician." He ran his hand through close-cropped blond hair and snapped, "I'm damned busy today, so how about telling me what you want?"

"Was
Della Wakefield your patient?"

"Look, officer..."

"Sergeant. Detective Sergeant Simon Threadneedle." He flipped open his identification wallet and held it out.

Weiman barely glanced at it. "Sergeant, medical records are confidential. I suggest you get a court order before you waste my time."

"Mrs. Wakefield is hardly in a position to object to anything you can tell me. She was murdered last night. Was she your patient?"

Weiman nodded. "It's Miss Wakefield. She'd never

married." He sighed, then leaned forward and used the intercom to tell someone to bring him Della Wakefield's chart.

If she was unmarried, why did she have a wedding ring? Simon wondered. A family heirloom? While they waited, Threadneedle asked, "How long have you been treating her?"

"Only since I bought the practice from Dr. Fenwick, about seven months."

The nurse brought in the file and Threadneedle waited patiently while Weiman perused it. When the doctor finally looked up, he asked, "What was wrong with her? Did she list a next of kin?"

"Only a great-niece, Marcia Sonnenburg," Weiman said, answering the last question first. "She was suffering from advanced rheumatoid arthritis in both ankles, knees, hips and in her lower spine. Also, she was in the early stages of congestive heart failure. I tried to convince her to go into a nursing home but she refused."

"What else can you tell me about her?"

"Not much. I've only seen her a couple of times." He smiled. "She was a talker. Chattered the whole time I was examining her."

"What did she talk about?"

"Nothing, everything. Just gossip, mostly about her neighbors." He shrugged. "I never paid any attention."

After leaving the doctor's office, Threadneedle picked up a Big Mac and Coke at McDonald's and ate in the parking lot, mulling over what he'd learned while he chewed. He's try the niece again when he got back to the office but first he'd check out some of the crossed out names from the address book. Eloise Hartshorn's address was only a few blocks away. He'd try there first.

The house was a small bungalow, its stucco faded and cracked, the tiny lawn patchy and brown. Threadneedle climbed the cracked cement steps and knocked on the peeling door frame. A quavering voice asked, "Who's there?" and Threadneedle identified himself. The door opened the length of a security chain and faded blue eye peered at him. "What you want?"

"I'm looking for Eloise Hartshorn."

The door closed, there was the sound of the chain being released, then the door re-opened. The voice belonged to an stooped, elderly man who peered up at Threadneedle with myopic eyes. "You're five months to late. My wife's buried up at Cypress Grove. What did you want to see her about?"

"Miss Wakefield."

"Della?" His eyes narrowed. "Della didn't send you here. She was at Ellie's funeral."

"Miss Wakefield is dead. We found your wife's name in her address book. We were hoping she could tell us something about Della Wakefield."

Hartshorn stepped back and turned around. "Don't know how much help I can be, but I guess you can come in."

Threadneedle closed the door and followed the old man into the living room. Except for a new leather recliner positioned in front of a television set and an old fashioned secretary, the furnishings were straight out of the fifties.

Taking a seat on the plastic-covered couch, Threadneedle pulled out a pen and notebook. "How well did you know Miss Wakefield?"

"I didn't know her at all. Met her maybe half a dozen times in the last thirty years. To tell you the truth, I couldn't stand her. All she ever did was gossip. Yakity-yak. At the funeral was the first time I'd seen her in, I guess, ten years. She was crippled up and didn't get around much."

"But she kept in touch with your wife?"

"Yep. They went to school together. For a while, they met for lunch most every week, but the last few years they kept in touch by mail. Della was quite a letter-writer. They both were. They wrote every week."

Threadneedle's heartbeat quickened. "I don't suppose you'd still have any of those letters?"

The old man gestured toward the secretary. "Ellie kept all her correspondence there. I ain't got around to cleaning it out. You're welcome to look."

The front of the secretary let down to form a writing surface and inside were pigeon holes filled with neatly tied bundles of envelopes. The envelopes in the largest bundle bore Della

Wakefield's return address.

"Do you mind if I take these?" Threadneedle asked. "I'll give you a receipt and they'll be returned as soon as we go through them."

Back at the station, Threadneedle tossed the letters on his desk and tied again to reach Marcia Sonnenburg. There was still no answer. With a sigh, he untied the bundle of letters, selected the oldest one, dated ten months earlier, and began to read.

Dear Ellie,

This has been a very boring week, nothing much happening on the block. The only interesting thing is that Miss Librarian bumped into that nice-looking young architect I told you about. Literally bumped into him on the street and they talked for a few minutes. At least he talked, she just stood there with her head down. It's too bad they're both so shy. They made such a good-looking couple, standing there on the street.

Mr. Meany came home drunk again and slapped his wife around. Really, that man should be arrested. I don't know how she puts up with him. I'm afraid for her. Someday he may kill her in one of his rages.

Oh, there is a new tenant in the Yuppie apartment. She's a pretty blonde in her early thirties. I think I'll call her Blondie. I do wish I knew their real names, I'm running out of new ones.

Hope both you and Horace are well.

Threadneedle replaced the letter in the envelope, and went one to the next one.

Well, Ellie, lots of news this week. Blondie isn't a real blonde and I'm very suspicious of her. She goes out about ten every night and is never home at two in the morning when I go to bed. And the clothes she wears! Little bitty skirts and those black fishnet stockings.

Architect has a kitten! He plays with it every morning and again in the evening and slips out of his office several times during the day to check on it. Such a nice man!! I do wish he and Miss librarian could get together.

And, surprise, surprise! Miss Snooty is a secret drinker! Always so hoity-toity, not speaking to anybody and Mrs. Ho at the grocery says she's terribly rude. Well, she keeps a bottle in her knitting bag. She rearranged her apartment when she got that new television and now she sits in front of the window. She drinks nearly a half a bottle every night.

I think there's something fishy about that accountant, too. I'm going to keep my eye on him.

My arthritis has been bothering the last few days but other than that I'm doing fine. Tell Horace to try some Fisherman's Friend drops for his cough.

The next few letters were in the same vein and he began skimming them until the third paragraph of a letter written just a month before Eloise Hartshorn's death. He read it twice and set it aside.

He was down to the last three letters when Cully returned. Cully dropped into a chair and pulled out a notebook. "I saw Reverend Beldan first. Wakefield was a member of his congregation, but she hadn't been to services in a couple of years. Once a year, she mailed a donation of twelve dollars, always one dollar bills. He visited her once a month and delivered a food basket. Never stayed long, he says."

Threadneedle's left eyebrow rose and he stroked his chin. "They didn't gossip?"

"Apparently not. He said she was uncommunicative, but he assumed it was because she was ashamed of taking what she termed 'charity'."

He flipped a page in his notebook. "Elizabeth Moore. She's a nurse. Wakefield was hospitalized a few years ago with pneumonia. Moore took care of her and they've exchanged cards. Moore used to drop by occasionally, but hasn't visited in almost a year."

Threadneedle tossed photocopies of the address book across the desk. "I've had better luck. Marcia Sonnenburg is a great-niece. Haven't been able to contact her yet. Alvin Weiman was her doctor. Eloise Hartshorn was an old school friend and correspondent." He tapped the letters on his desk.

"Wakefield was a gossip, but she did her gossiping by mail." He picked up the letter he had set aside. "Listen to this."

Ellie, you won't believe what a shocking week this has been. You know I can't breathe very well lying down anymore so I've been spending most of the night in my chair. Well, three nights this week, Blondie has brought a man home! Not only that, but a different man each time!

Then on Thursday evening I saw Dr. Kildare kissing that new nurse of his. And not just kissing, either. He had his hands all over her. Disgusting. And he has such a sweet looking wife. All I can say is, I'm glad he's not my doctor.

But that's not the worst. Old Bow Tie is a child molester. All this time, I thought those little girls he took up to his room were his granddaughters but now I'm not so sure. He took a little girl up yesterday and didn't pull his shade all the way down like he usually does. At first, I thought it might be her birthday or something because he brought out a cake and a bowl of something. Ice cream, I guess. After she ate, he took her on his lap and seemed to be reading to her, but then she went to sleep. He put her on the couch, took off her clothes and did the most unspeakable, unnatural things to her. I tell you, Ellie, it made me sick. I had to wheel myself into the bathroom and heave. If I had a phone, I'd have called the police.

"Old Bow Tie? Who the hell is that?" Cully asked taking the letter from Threadneedle's hand.

"Apparently Wakefield didn't know any of their names, so she made up ones based on some characteristic. Make a photocopy of that and let's get it down to Vice."

Cully left and Threadneedle picked up another letter and began to skim it, then stopped to re-read it.

This neighborhood is really going down hill! There was even a shooting last night! I'd dozed off so didn't see how it started. It must have happened in that disgusting bookstore because two men came running out and jumped in a red car and drove away. I'm sure one of them had a gun in his hand. I saw their license plate and wrote down the number. 459 EMB. I do wish I could afford a phone. Today there are men, police I suppose, going up and down the street talking to people. I do hope they'll come here.

I think I'll tell them about the accountant, too. Some pretty shady looking characters visit him at night. Why at night? It isn't tax season.

Oh, yes, I almost forgot in all the excitement. There are new tenants in the office across the street. They moved some really swanky furniture and the woman in charge looks like one of those people in the fashion magazines. Very elegant. I think I'll call her Miss Swanky. One room is full of telephones and computers. I wonder what kind of business it is.

Threadneedle looked up as Cully returned. "Remember that robbery at the porn shop a few weeks ago? Wakefield got the license number of the car. How come we missed her when we were canvassing the neighborhood?"

Cully took the letter and read it. "I think Carmichael was handling that case. I'll make a copy and drop it off on my way out. It's after five and I'm calling it a day. You coming?"

"Not yet. Sonnenburg may work. I'll hang around and try her again."

After Cully left, Threadneedle tried Sonnenburg again without success, then turned back to the letters and began making notes. His gut told him Wakefield had been killed by someone mentioned in the letters. The old woman had seen something that posed a threat to someone. Threat enough to warrant killing her. Bow Tie, the pedophile? The doctor to hide his affair? Miss Snooty to protect her secret? Who were the accountant's 'shady' clients? The hooker or one of her johns, someone who didn't want to be recognized? The wife beater? Or the wife? Miss Librarian or the architect?

He left the office at eight without reaching Sonnenburg. The next morning, he and Cully began canvassing the neighborhood. They started with Mrs. Ho at the corner grocery. They learned nothing new about Mrs. Wakefield, but Mrs. Ho was able to put a name to Bow Tie. Clarence Dobbs. And Miss Swanky was Elizabeth Conners, an investment counselor. Mrs. Ho had invested with her. A very nice lady, very smart, very sophisticated.

By the time they'd reached the end of the block, they'd met the architect, Dwight Summers; the hooker, Terry Dean; the abused wife (she was sporting a black eye and bruises on her wrists), Billy Sue Puckett and identified her husband, Mr. Meany, as George Allen Puckett; and the accountant, Ruben

Greenberg. None admitted to knowing Della Wakefield. None had seen any unusual activity in Wakefield's building. Miss Librarian and Miss Snooty obviously worked during the day.

They made their last call on Miss Swanky, Elizabeth Conners. She was indeed an elegant woman, in her mid-thirties, with a pleasant, open manner, but Threadneedle wasn't impressed. Her eyes were too small and too close together.

"Della Wakefield. The name does ring a bell but I don't believe she's a client. Let me check my files."

She left the room and Threadneedle to the opportunity to pick up a brochures. He'd glanced through it while he waited. It was the same brochure he'd seen in Wakefield's apartment and seemed to be touting some kind of tax-exempt bonds. Something about public housing for the homeless. He stuffed it in his pocket when Conners returned with a file.

"I was right, she isn't a client. She was on our mailing list and received our initial letter. She responded by letter requesting more information. We sent her a packet three weeks ago but I haven't had time to follow up."

"You never met her?"

"No."

When they left, Threadneedle was rubbing his chin. He glanced at Cully and asked, "Why would an old woman who couldn't afford a telephone want investment information?"

Cully shrugged and left to check more of the names from the address book. Threadneedle returned to the grocery store. He had to wait until Mrs. Ho finished waiting on a wizened little man, then asked, "Did you ever notice Mrs. Wakefield wearing a brooch of any kind?"

Mrs. Ho nodded. "Beautiful. A bar pin. One large ruby in the center and rose cut diamonds in the bar. Very old, very valuable. She never without it. Wore it always."

Threadneedle frowned. "Are you sure it wasn't costume jewelry?"

Mrs. Ho's eyes glittered. "Oh, no. It was a Burmese ruby. Very fine stone." At Threadneedle's skeptical look, she continued, "My father dealt in precious gems before the war, before we leave China. I learn early to know gems. Also, one time she tell me it was gift from fiancé. He send it to her from India, just before he killed."

He left the store with a line drawing and a full description of the pin. Back at the station, he had photocopies of the drawing sent to all of pawnbrokers in the city. He tried Sonnenburg again without success.

Two drive-by shootings, an armed robbery, a suspicious suicide, the rape and murder of a real estate agent and the finding of a decomposed body of a man in an abandoned building took most of Threadneedle's attention during the next week. He did find time to run a check on Ruben Greenberg and the accountant came up clean. Vice busted the hooker, Terry Dean, and were keeping an eye on Clarence Dobbs.

On the following Monday, Sonnenburg finally answered her phone and sounded genuinely shocked when Threadneedle told her of her great-aunt's murder. She agreed to stop by the station when she came up to arrange for the funeral and to bring any letters from Wakefield.

Threadneedle leafed through the Wakefield file, studying his notes. Something nudged the back of his brain but he couldn't bring it into focus. He pulled out the packet of letters and began re-reading them. One paragraph in the last letter that caught his attention.

You know I've never known what to do with Papa's ill-gotten gains, but I think I've finally found a way to make good use of it and provide for Marcia as well.

Threadneedle closed the file and folded his hands on top of it, racking his brain for an elusive memory. Then it came to him. He pulled the phone book from his desk drawer, looked up a number and dialed.

It was Wednesday afternoon when Marcia Sonnenburg entered Threadneedle's office. She was a tall woman in her forties with short-cropped brown hair and cold blue eyes. She was wearing a brown pant-suit and a yellow blouse with a lace jabot.

When she was seated, Threadneedle took a card from his pocket and began to read. "You have the right to remain silent..."

Threadneedle and Cully were having a beer in the back booth at Jaspar's when Carmichael joined them. "Thanks for the tip on that porno hold-up. We traced the car, brought the guy and a couple of his buddies in for a line-up and the clerk id'd them.

"I hear you got the niece for whacking the Wakefield woman. Thought she was from out of town. How'd you tie her in?"

"First, I asked myself why someone with so little obvious income would be interested in investments. Sonnenburg was her only relative so I did a little checking. Sonnenburg left for a vacation in Mexico the day Wakefield was killed. According to airline records, she was in town four hours between flights. Plenty of time to get out to her aunt's apartment.

"Wakefield liked to gossip. I figured if she gossiped to an old friend, she probably gossiped to her niece. In one of her letters to Hartshorn, she mentioned her father's ill-gotten gains. I remembered the savings account."

Cully interrupted, "But it had only a little over a hundred dollars."

"True. I called the bank. Wakefield had a safe deposit box with Marcia Sonnenberg. I got a court order to look in the box. There was over a million dollars in cash and bearer bonds.

Then I did a background check on Wakefield. Her father was Anson Wakefield, one of the biggest bootleggers in the city back during prohibition. He was reputed to be worth millions when he died back in '69."

"Yeah, but Wakefield was dying. Sonnenberg only had to wait a few months and whatever the old man left would have been hers."

"She denies it, but I think Wakefield wrote about her plans to invest the money with Elizabeth Conners. Sonnenburg was afraid the old woman was about to throw the money away in some get-rich-quick scheme and panicked."

"But you arrested her the minute she walked in!"

"She was wearing Wakefield's ruby brooch."

* * * *

Eyes

DAN ELLIS could feel the cold of the concrete floor creeping through him. The smell of alcohol choked him. He struggled to sit up but his body refused to obey him. His heart began to race. His ears picked up a faint rustling sound. He arched his neck and searched the shadows above the hanging florescent light. A pair of green eyes stared down at him from the darkness.

Panic welled up in him as more and more eyes appeared. Pleading eyes, pain-filled eyes, terrified eyes, eyes filled with hate. He opened his mouth and began to scream. Furry paws reached out and began to shake him.

"Dan. Wake up, Dan."

The shaking stopped as he opened his eyes. Long blond hair brushed his biceps as red nails bit into his flesh. His heartbeat slowed as he looked up into the petulant face.

"Karen." His voice was a dry croak. The sheets clung to his sweat soaked body as he pushed himself into a sitting position. "I guess I had a nightmare."

"Yeah? You have these bad dreams often?"

"No...yes...hell, I don't know. Sometimes."

"Well, I don't need a lover that wakes up screaming! You scared the bejasus out of me."

She flounced off the bed and he watched the smooth play of her buns as she stalked into the bathroom and slammed the door.

He swung his legs off the bed and reached for a cigarette. His hand trembled as he lit it. "Bitch," he mumbled. Well, let her go. There were plenty more chicks out there.

The alarm went off, startling him so badly that he dropped the cigarette. He grabbed for it with his left hand, his right hand fumbling to shut of strident buzz. The clock fell over and bounced off the nightstand. He kicked it in frustration, then yelped at the pain as his big toe connected. The buzzing stopped.

Dan shrugged into the black silk oriental robe he wore when he had overnight guests and stomped into the kitchen. He hunted through the cabinets for the can of coffee before he remembered he was out. Shit. Finding a dusty jar of instant coffee in the back of a cabinet, he ran a cup of hot water from the tap, stirred in a heaping teaspoon of coffee and took a swallow. He grimaced at the taste but forced himself to drink it. He was rinsing the cup when he heard the front door slam.

Carrying the coffee into the bathroom, he glanced around in disgust. "Bitch," he mumbled again as picked up the wet towels from the floor and wiped the hair and drops of makeup out of the lavatory.

He felt better when he climbed out of the shower and rubbed himself down briskly. Bloodshot eyes stared back at him as he shaved. He winced at his haggard face. This morning he looked ten years older than his thirty-two years.

It was the nightmares. They were ruining his sex life, driving him crazy. If they kept on, he'd have to break down and see a doctor. Maybe some of the stuff at the lab was poisoning him. Lord knew, it did certainly did weird things to the animals.

The cold, crisp air perked him up as he walked out to car. As he did almost every day, he stopped for a moment to admire the sleek lines of the Porsche. The car, even more than his seductively furnished luxury apartment, elegant clothes and extensive stereo equipment symbolized the life of his dreams.

By the time he reached the lab, he had forgotten the nightmare. He had spent the drive mentally thumbing through his address book. He decided he'd call the redhead he'd met last week at his favorite singles bar.

HE COULD feel the cold of the concrete floor creeping through him. The smell of alcohol choked him. He struggled to sit up but his body refused to obey him. His heart began to race. His ears picked up a faint rustling sound. He arched his neck and searched the shadows above the hanging florescent light. A pair of green eyes stared down at him from the darkness.

"Hey, knock it off you big ape. What's the matter with you?"

He struggled out of the nightmare. Green eyes stared down at him and he screamed in terror. The light clicked on. The redhead stared at him, her green eyes large and angry.

"Sorry," he panted. "I guess I had a bad dream."

"Yeah, I guess you did. Are you okay now?"

"Sure. Sorry if I scared you. Must have been something I ate."

"Hey, now just a damned minute."

He managed a weak grin. "I meant the seafood at that lousy restaurant."

"Well, if fish gives you that kind of dreams, maybe you'd better stick to steak."

She slid off the bed and reached for her clothes.

"Hey, come on back to bed."

"No thanks. It's almost six and I'm wide awake."

He sat up and reached for his robe as she finished dressing. He ran a hand through his tousled blond hair.

"Well, look, how about dinner tonight?"

"I don't think so." She paused at the bedroom door. "Look, I know it's none of my business, but I really think you should see someone about those nightmares."

He glared at her. "You're right. It's none of your business."

The look of pity she cast at him as she slipped out the door cut him like a knife. He sank down on the edge of the bed and fumbled for a cigarette. Should he seek help, he wondered. Was he going crazy? Maybe it was the booze. Look what it had done to his old man. Screaming out his last days in a Detox center tormented by demons only he could see. No, it couldn't be the booze. He didn't drink that much. Just social drinking when he was on the prowl. He wasn't a solitary drinker. He didn't put away a bottle at time like his old man. It couldn't be the booze. Or could it?

He stabbed out the cigarette. Okay. No more booze. He'd stick to white wine from now on.

Friday, he felt on top of the world as he drove to work. His thoughts centered on Patty Nelson. He'd been pursuing her for weeks without success. Then he learned she was a skiing fanatic. He'd finally broken down her resolve and enticed her with a three day skiing trip. Whistling Lara's Theme and picturing Patty seductively stripping out of ski pants, he pulled on his lab coat and headed for the animal room.

His shoulders ached and he stretched. The silence of the building made him look at his watch and he swore. Six o'clock and he was supposed to pick Patty up at seven-thirty. He didn't want to blow this weekend by being late.

He walked around the table to the row of cages that lined the wall. In one of the cages a white rabbit writhed in agony. All of the others had died earlier in the afternoon but this little bastard had hung on, hour after hour, twitching and whimpering. Why wouldn't the damned thing die? He couldn't complete his notes and leave until it did.

He walked back around the table, bumping his thigh against the corner as he squeezed between the table and the cat cages. Another irritation. The cat experiments weren't supposed to start until Tuesday and they had delivered sixteen cats yesterday morning. For the last two days he'd had to clamber around those extra damned cages.

He never thought of the hundreds of animals that suffered agony and death at his hands so that women could have a new shade of makeup or a different hair spray. As long as the cosmetics industry was willing to shell out the fees that enable him to support his swinging lifestyle, he didn't care what happened to the animals. They were only a medium in which to perform the requested tests. That there were other medium such as egg membranes, tissue cultures and more that would give more accurate results, that many of the test results were worthless didn't concern him. He wasn't being paid to make suggestions, just perform the tests. If those tests required the mutilation, torture and death of animals, then that's what the clients got.

But this batch of cats were getting to him. He'd done plenty of cat experiments before and they had never bothered him, but he'd come to hate these. He looked at them now. Most were sleeping, a few grooming themselves, one using a litter pan. Their cages crammed in behind the table where he worked made him feel claustrophobic.

Suddenly the emptiness of the building made him uncomfortable. The secretaries and other research assistants were all long gone. Since a security guard had inadvertently shut off all the oxygen to a whole row of isolation cages suffocating the animals and ruining an experiment, guards were forbidden to enter the labs. They only patrolled the grounds now. There was a forsaken, hollow feeling to the building and he felt the hairs on his neck rise.

Right now, he thought, he'd even welcome the bland moon face and garrulous inanities of Jess Ringold. Jess was the guard that had ruined the monkey experiments and Dan considered him little more than a cretin.

Dan jumped as across the room the rabbit gave a strangled scream. The animal gave a last shuddering twitch and died. Dan heaved a sigh of relief and rushed to the cage. He picked up his notebook, entered the time and his final notes. Tagging the body, he carried it into the next room and deposited it in the freezer with the other bodies. He would do the autopsies next week.

Dan's thoughts were on the pleasures he planned to extract from Patty Nelson's body over the weekend as he reentered the lab. His glance made a perfunctory sweep around the room as he unbuttoned his lab coat. It swept over the cat cages, hesitated and locked in on the end cage. The door was open and the cage was empty.

"Oh, shit. Come on, you bastard. Where are you? Kitty...kitty..."

From the top of the supply cabinet in the far corner of the room, two green eyes glared down at him.

He eased between the table and the cages and reached up. His hands paused momentarily as the big black tomcat spit at him. He reached again and then jerked back at the swipe of a paw, the claws leaving a bloody track across the back of his hand.

Dan swore, made another grab for the cat and missed as it launched itself over his head and landed on the table in the center of the room.

"Come on, damn it. I don't have time for this," he said through gritted teeth.

He made a furious dive for the cat and knocked over the tall steel stool, bruising his shin. The cat leaped to the top of the empty rabbit cages and then, with a swish of its long tail, sailed up onto the metal hood of the four foot light fixture over the table.

It sat there, seeming to grin at Dan, and began to wash a front paw.

Dan climbed clumsily onto the table, his leg beginning to ache and throb. A bottle of alcohol tottered and fell, shattering as it hit the floor. The fumes made his eyes water as he craned his neck, trying to locate the cat.

The black body, merging into the shadows seemed the size of a panther rather than a house cat. Standing on tiptoe, he stretched up. His fingers touched the silky fur and slid away as the cat stood up. Off balance, he teetered on the edge of the table.

The cat suddenly leaped. Dan yelled as the cat landed on his head. The weight of the cat threw him farther off balance. Arms windmilling, he fell backwards. His neck came down across the steel legs of the stool, crushing his fourth and fifth cervical vertebrae, tearing the spinal cord. His head bounced and slammed onto the floor.

Dan could feel the cold of the concrete floor creeping through him. The smell of alcohol choked him. He struggled to sit up but his body refused to obey him. His heart began to race. His ears picked up a faint rustling sound. He arched his neck and searched the shadows above the hanging florescent light. A pair of green eyes stared down at him from the darkness.

Panic welled up in him as more and more eyes appeared. Pleading eyes, pain-filled eyes, terrified eyes, eyes filled with hate.

He pulled his glance down and saw the cat sitting on his chest. Its purring seemed to reverberate throughout his body. He opened his mouth and screamed.

The cat sat up and lifted a paw. Hypnotized like a bird by a snake, he watched the cat flex its paw, the long nails gleaming. He could almost feel them tearing through his eyes, shredding lids, corneas. His scream rose to a howl of terror.

The paw flicked out and, claws sheathed at the last moment, gently slapped Dan's nose. The action was so reminiscent of a mother gently chastising a child that Dan was shocked into silence. The cat seemed to smile at him in approval.

There was a rustling noise above him and Dan looked back towards the ceiling. In the darkness beyond the reach of the light, more eyes appeared. Bodies began to materialize around the eyes. They filled the upper reaches of the room. Brown eyes of monkeys driven insane; mutilated, pink, pain-filled eyes of rabbits; the frightened yet trusting eyes of dogs that had once been someone's cherished pet; mouse and rat eyes filled with pain and terror. Eyes pleading, begging to be relieved of their agony.

He looked back at the cat on his chest. The green eyes seemed to gleam with an unholy delight as it slowly stood up and stretched.

Dan's eyes followed the cat's paws as it stepped down onto his arm. Those paws were suddenly familiar.

Dan sighed with relief. This was only the now familiar nightmare. It wasn't really happening, it couldn't be. He closed his eyes and waited to wake up.

DR. MICHAEL Mossman, the medical examiner, leaned back and picked up his coffee cup before answering Detective Carruthers.

"There's no real question as to the cause of death. Dan Ellis died of a broken neck." He paused, frowned, and then shook his head. "There was some cyanosis that initially indicated smothering but we finally ruled that out. There was nothing in his nostrils or trachea but a few hairs from the belly of a cat."

He chuckled and looked up at the detective. "Never heard of anyone using a cat to smother someone. Have you?"

The big detective joined in the laughter. "Can't say that I have, Doc."

* * * *

See Skeeter Run

"YOU DON'T love me." Bitsy Blue slammed the plate on the table sending green olives skittering across the black and white oilcloth.

Skeeter threw out a hand catching two of the olives before they could hit the floor. Popping them in his mouth, he reached for the bologna and onion sandwich tottering on the edge of the plate. "Now, Babe—"

"Don't you 'Babe' me. If you loved me, you'd marry me." Pushing a wisp of long blonde hair off her cheek, Bitsy stomped the three steps to the refrigerator, jerked open the door and pulled out a can of beer. "Well, let me tell you something, buster, I've had enough."

Skeeter reached for the can, but Bitsy held it above her head, just out of his reach. His gaze swept up over her flat stomach, tiny waist and paused on her out thrust breasts. He risked a glance at her face.

Anger flashed in her blue eyes. He dropped his gaze and concentrated on the sandwich in front of him. It never paid to argue with Bitsy when she was in this kind of mood.

"I'm sick of waiting on you," she said, shaking the can at him.

Skeeter took a bite of the sandwich. Best to just ignore her. Let her get it out of her system. He took another bite.

"You ain't listening to me." She pulled the tab. Foam bubbled up, ran down over her hand and dripped on the back of Skeeter's shirt. "Oh, hell. Look what you made me do."

She tossed the can of beer in the rust-streaked sink, grabbed a towel and wiped her hand. "Well, you just better listen, Henry Drew, 'cause I mean it this time. You want the milk, you got to buy the cow."

Skeeter Drew choked, spraying bits of bread and meat. Dumping the rest of the sandwich back on the plate, he glared up at her. He'd better change the subject in a hurry. Bitsy never called him Henry unless she was really riled. "Look what you did! This is my last clean shirt!"

"Yeah? Tough titty. You want a clean one, you'll have to wash it yourself." Her gaze lit on the clock. "I'm gonna be late to work again. I got the early shift today." Without another word, she grabbed her purse and dashed out the door.

Skeeter picked up the sandwich and finished it, the fingers of his left hand drumming on the oilcloth. He pushed the plate away and leaned back in his chair. Bitsy had sounded serious this time. Maybe he should take off for a day or two. Better yet, a week or so. Let her have time to cool down, miss him, and forget this marriage business. He wasn't really running away. No, he was just making a temporary strategic retreat.

He ran a hand through his hair and smiled. Why not go to Mexico? He'd wanted to try his hand at deep sea fishing ever since Buddy had come back full of tales of cheap beer, fighting fish and hot women. Maybe Buddy's talk wasn't all bullshit. Now was the perfect time to check it out.

He stood up, stretching his five-feet-five body. He'd read somewhere that stretching regularly could add an inch or so to his height. So far it hadn't worked but he continued to do it out of habit.

He strode into the bedroom and began gathering his dirty clothes, stuffing them in a red canvas tote. Maybe one of those hot little Mexican women would wash them for him.

In the closet, he got down on his knees and felt for the loose baseboard at the back. His fingers found it and he lifted it out and set it aside. From the cavity, he removed a plastic bank bag. Replacing the baseboard, he carried his stash to the unmade bed.

He sat on the edge of the bed and emptied the bag onto the sheet. He shoved aside a couple of plastic bags of marijuana and began to count the money. One hundred and eighteen dollars. He counted it twice but the total remained the same. Not enough.

He stuffed the bills in his pocket and picked up the packets. Two ounces of Acapulco gold. He tossed them gently in his hands. Glancing at the watch on his freckled wrist, he grinned. Ten o'clock. Plenty of time. Artie Bragg would do half a dozen jobs for what was in those bags. He could even pull a couple himself. Catlow would buy all animals they could steal. Yeah. By tonight, he'd have another three or four hundred dollars. Then off to siestaville!

He put the Baggies in his pocket, picked up his tote and headed for the door. In the kitchen, he hesitated. Should he leave Bitsy a note? Let her know he had better things to do than put up with her tantrums? Hell, she was lucky to have a man like him. Wasn't he paying all the bills? Didn't he buy all the groceries, even buy her clothes? She didn't have to work in that crummy restaurant. Most girls would fight to get what he was giving her. Why he didn't even beat on her. Not even a little slap once in a while like most men did.

Nah. Let her worry. If he decided to come back, she'd be too glad to see him to press this marriage shit.

The dark blue van was scratched and dented, but the souped up engine purred like a well fed lion. He tossed the tote on the passenger seat and headed across town.

Artie was coming down the stairs as Skeeter entered the apartment building. He brushed by Skeeter, calling over his shoulder, "Can't stop now. Catch you later."

Skeeter dashed after him. "Wait. I need you to work this afternoon."

Artie waved a hand without looking back and broke into a run. Skeeter glared after him, noticing for the first time that Artie was decked out in a white shirt and bilious green sport coat. "What the hell you duded up for?" he called as Artie disappeared around the corner.

"Him and Darlene is getting married this afternoon," a youthful voice said.

Skeeter glared down at the kid sitting on the steps then stomped back to the van, shaking his head in disgust. Married. Artie had a good thing going with Darlene, why'd he want to spoil it by marrying her? And why today of all days?

Now he'd have to do all of the work himself. He rolled a toke, slammed the van in gear and headed towards the suburbs, then changed his mind. The rich bitches paid big money for the return of their "lost" fancy pets but he didn't have time to wait around to collect. He needed money today and that meant quantity rather than quality. Catlow paid cash on delivery.

Someday he was going to follow old Catlow and find out where he sold all the cats and dogs he bought. Then maybe he'd be able to cut Catlow out, supply them direct and increase his take. He hummed as he drove. Not today. He didn't have time, but when he got back. He chuckled, picturing Catlow's anger when he cut him out.

Four hours later, Skeeter was cruising up Diablo Drive, ready to quit when he saw the dog lying on the grass, a big golden retriever. It lifted its head and thumped its tail as he pulled to the curb. A quick glance up and down showed him a deserted street.

Crossing the sidewalk, he murmured to the dog in a friendly voice and extended his hand. The tail thumped rapidly but the dog didn't move. Skeeter left the sidewalk and moved across the lawn. The dog stood up and sniffed the outstretched hand. Skeeter scratched the dog's ears then slid his hand down and under the collar. He began coaxing the dog across the yard. The dog came willingly enough until they neared the sidewalk, then he pulled back, whining.

"Come on, boy. Just a little farther and I'll give you a nice big bone. Now stop that. Oh shit, look what you did, you bastard." The dog had begun to growl and snap, leaving a trail of broken skin across Skeeter's wrist. Twisting the collar into a choke hold, he picked up the dog and carried him to the back of the van. As Skeeter shoved him inside, the collar came off in Skeeter's hand and the dog threw himself against the closing door but not in time to escape.

From up the street he heard a voice yelling. He glanced over his shoulder and saw a kid running toward him. He jumped in the van and burned rubber as he raced away. Thank God he'd remembered to smear mud on the license plate. Not enough to get him stopped but enough to make reading the plate difficult.

Rummaging in the glove compartment as he drove, Skeeter found a rag. It was gray and grungy but it would have to do. He wrapped it around his bleeding wrist and used the dog collar to fasten it in place. As he was struggling to fasten the buckle, his glance lit on one of the metal tags. Lipshitz. What kind of name was that for a dog?

Catlow's place was a half dozen ramshackle buildings in the hills a dozen miles outside of town. The chain link fence that encircled them was the newest and best looking thing on the place. Skeeter opened the gate and drove in. He honked and a moment later Catlow came out of the house carrying a bundle of leashes in one hand and a large animal carrier in the other.

As Skeeter climbed out of the truck, Catlow spit a stream of tobacco juice into the dust. "What you got for me today?"

"Nine dogs and three cats."

Catlow shoved the carrier at Skeeter. "Get them cats out. Then we'll leash the dogs."

Skeeter slid open the side door just far enough to wiggle inside. Getting the cats was no problem because when he'd first started in the pet-napping business, he'd installed a wire cage just inside the side door. Pulling on a pair of heavy leather gloves, he quickly transferred the cats from the cage to the carrier, backed out and slammed the door.

"Now, let's get them dogs."

Keeping a tight hand on the handle of the carrier, he shook his head and said, "Uh uh. Money first."

"Now see here, I got to see what I'm buying."

Skeeter just grinned. First time he'd done business with Catlow, the old man had deliberately let one of the dogs loose then refused to pay him for that one, claiming since it was running loose on his place, it must belong to him. Now Skeeter demanded payment before the dogs were let out of the truck.

Old man Catlow went through his usual arguments, but Skeeter leaned against the truck and grinned, waiting for the old man to run down. Out of the corner of his eye, Skeeter saw a plume of dust approaching down the dirt road.

"Looks like someone's coming," he said.

"All right, all right." Catlow said, pulling out his wallet and counting out the money. "Get them critters out and get out of here."

Skeeter unlocked the back door. Before he could brace himself, Lipshitz hit the door, slamming it into Skeeter and knocking him off balance. All nine dogs bounded out of the truck, racing around the yard and barking. From the buildings, other dogs joined in an ear-splitting canine chorus.

To hell with it. Like Catlow said, the dogs were on his

property, so they were his. Skeeter had his money so Catlow could worry about catching them. Ignoring the old man's yells for help, Skeeter jumped back into the van and headed across the yard.

A late model station wagon with lettering on the side had stopped just outside the gate. He read the words HEALTH DEPARTMENT before the door opened and two women and man got out. Skeeter rolled down his window and yelled, "Open the gate!"

The man complied, and Skeeter barreled through. As he raced up the road, he glanced in the mirror in time to see a bundle of golden fur flash out of the gate, knock one of the women sprawling, and streak away through the sagebrush.

Skeeter leaned out the window and yelled, "Run, Lipshitz, run." He laughed and gunned the motor, throwing up a cloud of dust that hid the escaping dog, and barely missing another vehicle with HUMANE SOCIETY on the door.

SKEETER STOPPED that evening in Tijuana and started hitting the bars. He got into a poker game with a couple of locals and some sailors from San Diego. At first it was just a friendly game. He won a few small pots and lost a few bigger ones. Then Lady Luck had decided to sit in his lap. He won several big pots. The sailors took their losses in such good part that he'd given them each a ten-spot to get back to base.

Feeling flush and on top of the world, Skeeter hung around for a couple more drinks before leaving the bar in a happy but none to steady haze. He started up the dark street towards his van filled with a mild euphoria.

Half way back to his vehicle, two figures charged out of the shadows. Starlight glinting on bare steel shocked Skeeter out of his daze. He ducked, threw a shoulder into the man in front of him sending him toppling to the ground and began to run for his life.

A group of college students rounded the corner, taking up the whole sidewalk. Skeeter managed to dash around them, putting them between himself and his pursuers. He unlocked the van, jumped in and locked the door before the two men broke free of the group.

He grinned with nervous relief as the motor roared to life. He swung away from the curb, barely missing the angry men and headed east on the highway to Mexicali.

Once out of town, he rolled down the window and let the cool desert air blow away the alcohol and fear. It wasn't that he was chicken, he told himself. It was just that he was a lover, not a fighter. "He who runs away, lives to love another day," he paraphrased aloud. Two hours later, he pulled the van off the road, took a leak, then crawled in back and went to sleep.

The next day he passed through Mexicali and turned south, stopping for lunch in San Felipe, then continuing south to the small fishing village Buddy had told about.

DAVID GREENBAUM sat on the couch looking at the news on television without really seeing it. It was stupid to get so attached to a dumb animal but he really missed Lipshitz. He'd called all of the animal shelters, not that he'd had much hope. Bobby Mason had seen the man put the dog into the back of his van and drive off. The thought of Lipshitz being tortured in some medical experiment made him queasy.

He finished the wine in his glass and picked up the bottle from the floor. He'd just started to pour another glass when he heard a scratching at the front door. He put the glass and bottle on the floor and crossed the room. The last thing he needed right now was to deal with some salesman or a couple of religious nuts.

He jerked open the door. Two golden paws slammed into his shoulders, knocking him back a step. A wet tongue began to wash his face.

"Lipshitz!"

Tears ran unheeded down his face and he hugged the dog.

THE LITTLE Mexican town wasn't much to look at, just a couple of dirt streets, a collection of shacks, a dilapidated wharf, and a few fishing boats. But the people were friendly, the women willing, the Tecate beer cold and everything surprisingly cheap. For weeks, Skeeter rarely left the Cantina, except to climb the outside stairs to his room.

He'd made a connection for some cheap, locally grown marijuana and with the money he'd won in Tijuana, was able to lay in a stash to take back with him. This trip had been a smart idea. He was having a ball and now he'd have a nice stake when he got home.

Buddy had been right. This place was paradise.

But even paradise can get old. One day in the fifth week of his stay, Skeeter awoke early, crawled out from under the mosquito netting and reached for his jeans. They were clean but wrinkled. He'd had no trouble finding a woman to wash his clothes, but she never ironed anything. Bitsy always ironed his clothes, even his jeans.

He dropped them on the floor and lay back down, staring at the slowly revolving ceiling fan. He really didn't feel well; his head ached and his stomach was queasy. Not that he was really sick. No. He was never sick. He'd just been drinking too much.

Suddenly, the thought of spending another day drinking in the Cantina downstairs depressed him. And, although he hated to admit it, he missed Bitsy. He'd been gone over a month, time enough for her to get her act together and forget the marriage shit.

He dressed and headed for the wharf. There was still one thing he wanted to do before he headed back to the States. Go deep sea fishing. Catch one of the really big ones. One like Jake had mounted over the bar at the CHUG-A-LUG.

Late that afternoon, Skeeter staggered off the boat, and leaning heavily on Pablo's arm, barely managed to make it up the rickety wharf, across the street and into the Cantina, where he collapsed on a chair. He'd never been so sick in his life. He was burning up, his head throbbed unbearably, his gut ached from repeated bouts of vomiting, and his thirst was tormenting.

Domingo, the bartender, slapped a bottle of beer on the table in front of him, but Skeeter shoved it away and said, "Water...agua," in a cracked voice. When the water came, he gulped it down. A moment later, he staggered to the door and retched in the street. He shuffled back, flopped on the chair, buried his head in his arms on the newspaper-strewn table, and closed his eyes.

A tear worked its way from under an eyelid and slid down his cheek. He was dying. He knew it. Dying. Alone and in a foreign country. Bitsy would never know what happened to him. No one would know.

A fly lit on his forehead and trod down across his eyelid. He blinked rapidly, and as it flew away, his gaze lit on the paper under his head. He blinked again and stared at the print. English. Slowly, he raised his head, still staring at the paper. The first English language paper he'd seen in a month. It was several weeks old but it was nice to see English words again. He struggled to focus his eyes and a caption leaped out, slamming into his brain. RABIES EPIDEMIC.

He sat up and began to read. He read the article three times but the only thing his brain grasped was that most of the animals at Catlow's place had been discovered to have had rabies and had been destroyed. Catlow had been arrested.

The yellow dog. The one he'd taken to Catlow. The one that had bitten him. His arm was still sore and swollen. Rabies. He had rabies! Skeeter dropped the paper and uttered a strangled cry. Rabies! People died from rabies!

He jumped up, sending the chair crashing to the floor. He had to get home. Bitsy would know what to do. Bitsy was smart. She wouldn't let him die.

He tottered out the door. With one hand braced against the adobe wall for support, he shuffled around back to the van and climbed in. He had to get home. Get to Bitsy. She'd take care of him.

It was a long, miserable drive. Only his panic kept him going. At the border, it was sheer terror that sharpened his dulled brain enough to tell the suspicious border guard that he merely suffering from a combination of Montezuma's Revenge and the mother of all hangovers. Maybe his glowing sunburn and cracked lips helped.

By the time Skeeter reached their apartment building, he was almost too weak to climb the stairs. His headache had turned into a full blown migraine and the stairs wavered and danced before his eyes. After falling twice, he crawled the rest of the way on hands and knees. His hands were shaking so bad it took him several tries before he finally got the door unlocked and open.

He pulled himself up and staggered across the living room. "Bitsy," he called. The sound of his voice reverberated in his head like a klaxon but only silence answered his call. He peered into the empty kitchen, then weaved his way into the bedroom. Bitsy wasn't home. Tears of self-pity streamed unheeded down his cheeks as he stumbled onto the bed and drifted into exhausted sleep.

He surfaced from nightmare-ridden dreams to the feel of damp coolness encompassing his face. The dog! The dog had come to finish him off! He tried to shove it away but his hand met only air.

"Get away", he screamed but the words came out in a raspy croak.

Bitsy's voice penetrated the fog in his brain. "Hush now."

"Don't let him get me!"

"Don't let who get you?"

"Lipshitz. Don't let him get me again."

"Who's Lipshitz?"

He struggled to sit up. The wet cloth tumbled onto his chest. He blinked and stared into Bitsy's face. For a moment he thought he saw concern in her eyes, but he must have imagined it for when he looked closer, he saw only anger.

She straightened and snapped, "Where the hell have you been?"

His own hackles began to rise, but then memory returned and with it, some of the panic that had driven him home. He swung his legs off the bed and tried to sit up. The room spun and he toppled back onto the bed. When the room stopped spinning, he reached for her hand. "I'm sorry, Babe. I just had some thinking to do."

"Bull shit. You ran away."

He needed her. At least for now. Somehow he had to pacify her. "I didn't. Honest, I didn't. I'd never run out on you."

"The hell you wouldn't. You're always running away. You ain't got no more backbone than a...a...an amoeba. You've never taken no responsibility and you never will!"

"That ain't so." He remembered why he'd taken off for Mexico, and forced a weak smile, knowing just how to get her to help him. "I went away to think about what you said, about marriage."

"Ha!"

The headache surged back full force. He groaned and closed his eyes. "It's true, Babe. I done a lot of thinking. You're right. We should get married. I wanted to get us a stake so we could do the thing right."

He opened one eye a slit to see how she took that statement. She was staring at him, mouth open. Then her eyes brightened. "You mean it, Skeeter? You ain't just saying it 'cause you're sick?"

Of course he was, but he'd play along for a while. "I mean it, Bitsy. As soon as I get well, we'll get married."

"So you got a stake?"

"Yeah. There's a half dozen bricks of marijuana hidden in the van. Soon as I'm on my feet again—"

"Shit, Skeeter, you know I hate that stuff."

"Now don't be that way. I'm real sick, Babe, but as soon as..." He groaned and opened his eyes. "You still got your library card?"

She nodded.

"Go get one of them medical books. Will you do that?"

"If you're really sick, you should go to a doctor."

"Nah. Just get one of them books. It'll say what to do. Probably just got some green beer." She hesitated, worry marring her face. "Just do it, Babe. Please. Sooner I get better, sooner we can get married."

He watched her leave the room and listened for the front door to close, then dragged himself into the bathroom. Back in bed, he dozed until she returned.

Handing him the book, she said, "I gotta go to work. Are you sure you'll be all right until I get off?"

"Yeah. You go ahead."

"If you ain't, I'm gonna get you to a doctor."

As soon as she was gone, he sat up and leafed through the book until he found the section on rabies. The words blurred and jumped around on the page as he tried to read.

Acute viral infection...result of a rabid
dog bite...human rabies usually fatal....
incubation period... four to eight weeks....
fever, headache...intense thirst...spasms
...killed and brain examined....

He let the book fall to the floor and screamed in pure terror. He had it. He had rabies. They killed animals to examine their brains. Did they kill humans, too? Examine their brains? His brains? He wasn't ready to die. Usually fatal. Usually. Maybe not always. The book didn't say always. He was too young to die. Bitsy would call in a doctor. If they knew he had it, they'd come for him. Open up his head to get at his brain. He had to get away. Run. Hide. Somewhere where they'd never find him.

He scrambled off the bed and stared dazedly around the room. Pack. He needed to pack his things. No. He'd left everything in Mexico. Just go. Now. Before they came for him. Run. Hide.

He staggered out of the apartment and down the stairs. He'd go to Catlow's place. Catlow was in jail. They'd never look for him there.

Outside, the bright sunlight blinded him. He leaned against the wall, eyes closed. A car backfired; once, twice. Footsteps pounded towards him. The noise of the street slammed into his aching head like miniature sledgehammers. The wail of a siren coming closer sent icy fingers scrambling up his spine. He opened his eyes. Up the street he saw flashing lights racing towards him. They were coming for him! Cut off his head...dig out his brain...run...he had to run...get away...run...The racing footsteps were closer. Next to him a woman screamed.

A howl of pure animal terror tore from his throat. He launched himself away from the wall and began to run. He slammed into another body. Something jammed into his stomach, exploded in a burst of agony.

BITSY BLUE chewed a knuckle as she listened to the detective. "...unfortunate accident...armed robbery at the liquor store...ran right into the robber...wild-eyed and screaming...plenty of witnesses. Any idea why he was running?"

"He was sick, burning up with fever when I left," Bitsy said.

The detective nodded. "The autopsy showed him to be suffering from septicemia. Apparently he'd suffered some kind of abrasion on one arm that had become infected. The bacteria had spread through his body. Too bad he didn't go to a doctor. Antibiotics could have cleared it up." He shook his head. "I wonder why he was running."

Bitsy looked up and sighed. "Who knows. Skeeter was always running."

* * * *

Escape

MARK CONNERS was scared. More than scared, he was terrified. He glanced in the rear view mirror for the tenth time in as many minutes. He didn't see the new 1980 Cadillac but he wasn't reassured. It was back there, somewhere. In his mind's eye, he could see the sneering face of Emilio Vasquez. And Emilio wouldn't be alone. Hell, no. Emilio was never alone. Mario and Chato stuck to Vasquez like burrs on a dog's tail.

Chato would be driving. The little punk thought he was another Mario Andretti whenever he got behind the wheel. Mark smiled. They were Californios. Chato wouldn't know about wet Washington weather, especially May weather. Maybe they'd spin out. Yeah! In his mind's eye he could see the big car fishtailing, slamming through a barrier, rolling, bursting into flames.

He savored the picture for a moment, then his smile faded.

Mario would be in the passenger seat, probably playing with his damned Uzi machine pistol. Of course, Vasquez would be in the back seat, guzzling beer from the limo refrigerator, and acting like some oil rich Arab.

Mark's stomach twisted. Emilio would have that damned machete on the seat beside him. Mario's gun didn't scare him all that much, he had a Colt 10 mm Delta Elite and three extra magazines that had belonged to his father and he was a better shot than Mario. No, the gun didn't worry him, but that machete...He shivered and swallowed the bile that rose and burned in the back of his throat.

Mark slammed a fist against the wheel, causing the car to swerve slightly. He over-corrected and fishtailed before he had the car under control again. Jesus, all he needed was an accident with ten kilos of cocaine in the trunk.

It had all seemed so easy during spring break in Acapulco.

And the initial part of his plan had worked; he and his buddy, Art, had hijacked the delivery in Los Angeles, the ten kilos was now in the trunk. What he hadn't planned for was Emilio Vasquez and his damned machete. Now, Art was back in Fresno, hacked into pieces and he, Mark Conners, was running for his life.

Well, he was on his own turf now. He'd lose them soon and when he'd sold the coke, he'd take off for good. He'd left a note telling his mother and that sanctimonious bastard she'd married that he was going away to live his own life and not to try and find him.

This whole thing was their fault. Always carping about his grades, his friends. Who needed them? Who needed college? He hadn't wanted to go to Tahiti; they'd dragged him there for Christmas vacation. And if they hadn't made him go, he'd never have seen the boat. They could have bought the boat for him out of the old man's pocket change, but no, he was supposed to earn it. Well, he was earning it now.

For a moment he forgot the Cadillac, forgot Emilio Vasquez while he pictured the boat and drifted into the fantasy that had occupied him for the past five months. The blue skies and bluer waters, the old sloop gliding into uncharted lagoons, going where he wanted, when he wanted. Nobody telling what to do. Escape.

The word echoed through his head, chasing away the dream. First he had to escape Vasquez. He glanced nervously in the mirror. Was that the Cadillac? He hunched forward, straining to see through the traffic behind him. His eyes blurred. He blinked rapidly, trying to erase the gritty feeling behind his lids. Sleep. He needed sleep. Well, he could sleep when he reached the mountain. He glanced in the mirror again. The Cadillac was just coming over the hill a few miles behind him. There was no mistaking that bilious green color or Chato's aggressive driving.

He began to sweat. Where the hell was the cutoff?

He nearly missed the exit ramp, took it too fast, hit a patch of sand on the road, spun out and slid sideways onto Highway 504 before he could bring the car to a stop.

Well, he was awake now! Gunning the motor, he charged up the two lane road and pulled into a spot where he could watch the freeway without being seen. Minutes, that seemed like hours later, he laughed aloud as the Cadillac passed the intersection racing north.

Still laughing, he pulled back onto the pavement and headed

into the mountains. The old logging road was so overgrown he almost passed it. No one would find him at the cabin on Mount St. Helens. He'd get the sleep his body craved. Tomorrow he'd meet the buyer in Castle Rock, collect his money, grab a flight from Portland to San Francisco and then—yes!—on to Tahiti. Tahiti and the boat. Freedom. Escape.

The cabin wasn't much, just one room but he hardly noticed. Dropping the backpack filled with cocaine on the floor, he stumbled towards the bed. He'd escaped! Vasquez would never find him. His mother and the nerd she'd married would never find him. His dad was too wrapped up in his new trophy wife to care if his only son disappeared. Free. Free, at last!

He giggled as he pulled off his boots. No more bullshit. Just blue skies, blue water...he'd paint the boat blue. Blue...the color of freedom, of escape.

Nerves, strung nearly to the breaking point during the all night drive, unwound like a snapped watch spring as he stretched out. Within seconds of hitting the pillow, he was dead to the world. Not even the erupting volcano penetrated his sleep. Two hours later, he was truly dead to the world, buried beneath a wall of volcanic mud and ash. Mark Conners had found his final escape.

* * * *

Bug off

IT WAS AFTER midnight when the rattling old Ford taxi clanked to a stop in front of the dusty and crumbling steps of the Carib Hotel. Reginald Coomba ran a quick hand over his kinky, graying hair and straightened his shoulders. Perhaps the late arrival would be an American. American tourists brought money and laughter and now they were beginning to return to Montego Bay. Not that many of them came to the Carib. Most went to Half Moon Bay or the newer resorts at Ocho Rios. White teeth gleamed in his dark chocolate face. Reginald liked Americans.

His smile of welcome faded as he watched the man approach the desk. The short cropped, blond hair, the rigid back and the arrogant glance that swept over Reginald and dismissed him was all too familiar. This was no American. Reginald stared into the night, his very posture radiating his dislike as the man registered.

"I want a front room with a balcony on the seventh floor." It wasn't a request. Reginald longed to be able to tell the arrogant bastard that all of the rooms were taken. With the hotel half empty, he didn't dare. Silently he picked up the key to 702 and laid it on the desk.

"Have my bags taken up and I want to be called at six-thirty in the morning."

Reginald glanced down at the registration form and smiled inwardly, pleased to be able to deny this guest something. "I'm sorry, Mr. Waller, but our bellman went off duty at midnight. I'm afraid you will have to carry your own bags."

The cold, blue gaze swept over Reginald making his skin crawl. If eyes were truly the mirror of the soul, this man had none. Reginald didn't need his mother's 'sight' to know evil when it was staring him in the face.

"You carry them," the man said.

"I'm sorry, but I am not allowed to leave the desk." Striving to maintain his dignity as a wave of fear washed over him, Reginald turned away and picked up a sheaf of nearby papers. He kept his back turned until he heard the elevator doors close and the ancient contraption began its laborious ascent.

WALLER FOUGHT down the rage that burned in him as the elevator creaked its way up. The clerk was a water beetle. He had seen it clearly as the man had laid his key on the desk. A big, black, ugly water beetle. A filthy, germ-ridden beetle that needed to be killed, squashed under his foot. Perhaps, before he left....

He shuddered. Bugs. They were everywhere, even invading his homeland. Suddenly the elevator reminded him of the small cellar room where his grandfather had hidden from the Allies, living out the last few years of his life is semi-darkness. As a child, Waller had been fascinated by tales of his grandfather. He'd hidden there one day, pretending to be his grandfather fighting to preserve the purity of his race, had fallen asleep on the musty, rotting cot. While he slept, the candle had guttered and he wakened in darkness with cockroaches crawling over his body.

The elevator groaned to a stop and Waller stepped out onto the threadbare carpet. The odor of mildew and dust assailed him. His nostrils flared in disgust.

He dumped his case on the sagging bed and surveyed the room. It was large but shabby with the neglected air of a decrepit dowager. An aged sofa sat against one wall flanked by a cigarette burn-scarred table and a chair. The orange upholstery was faded and stained with oil from a multitude of suntanned bodies.

Waller shuddered, crossed the room, slid open the glass door and walked out onto the balcony. He breathed slowly and deeply, letting the cool air calm his rage and disgust. Tomorrow he would meet with Castenada. He wondered briefly who Castenada wanted killed. Not that it mattered, he wished he could kill them all. The congestion, the noise, the stink. And their stupid superstitions. Voodoo. The memory of the old Haitian crept into his mind. Shivering, he forced the thought away. Silly superstition. He stretched and loosened his tie as he moved back into the room.

THE MERRY screams of children awakened Reginald Coomba. He lay for a moment listening to their happy play. From the kitchen came a low murmur of feminine chatter, the clatter of dishes. A surge of contentment flowed through him and he smiled. Life might be hard but it was still good.

He swung his long black legs over the edge of the bed and reached for a smoke. He removed the last cigarette and tossed the crumpled pack on the floor. He glanced towards the kitchen, retrieved the pack and laid it on the broken chair that served as a night table. His fingers gently straightened the cigarette. Should he smoke it now or wait until he had eaten? He reached for his pants and searched through the pockets, spilling the change onto the bed. Not enough for another pack. Carefully he laid the cigarette on the table. He'd wait.

His mother grinned a toothless smile as he walked into the kitchen, her fingers not pausing from the straw doll she was weaving. As he sat down at the table, Malia, his brother's widow, slid plate of red beans and rice in front of him, untied her apron and hurried off to her part time job.

After a glance at the battered clock, he ate rapidly. His double shifts at the hotel left little time for more than sleep and yet barely kept a roof over their heads and food on the table.

Without looking up, his mother said, "Davy done sold six dolls yesterday. Tol' de boy if'n he sold the same today, he could keep fifty cents. He most near got enough saved for that baseball glove he got his heart set on." She put down the doll and frowned. "Doan let Davy sell at the hotel today."

"Why not, Mama?"

She shrugged. "Bad feelin'. Evil be lurking. Boy, you hear?"

Reginald nodded silently, not really listening, his thoughts on Davy. Much as he loved his own daughters, his nephew, Davy, was his joy. The boy wasn't going to spend his life hawking straw to the tourists if Reginald could help it. At twelve, Davy already showed tremendous sports ability. Baseball could be a way out of the grinding poverty. The boy would have his glove.

WALLER WOKE even before the phone rang. Early morning was his favorite time of day. The day, the world, was clean and new then. He slipped into sweats and headed for the beach.

The sun was only a faint line along the horizon as he ran on the damp sand. An occasional wave licked tentatively at his Reeboks. He ran his usual five miles back and forth along the beach, before turning back toward the hotel. He felt vibrantly alive, charged with energy and all powerful.

The girl was half hidden in the shadow of the doorway. In her bright dress, she reminded him of a butterfly and he slowed. She beckoned and he felt the heat rise in his loins. He moved closer. She swayed towards him into a shaft of light, her arms lifted, her lips puckered seductively.

He recoiled in horror. He could see her clearly now. A spider. A black widow spider reaching for him, that hideous poisonous mouth so close. He dodged the threatening arms. Her left hand grasped against his arm. A silent scream rose in his throat. She'd *touched* him! Turning, he ran, unseeing, across the beach and into the water began to swim, trying to wash away the feel of her touch.

Within minutes reason returned and he treaded water while he studied the beach. No one was pursuing him. None of the few people moving about seemed to have noticed his panic. He began to swim again, parallel to the beach until he was opposite his hotel.

He walked dripping to the elevator, ignoring the desk clerk's call. In his room, he headed for the shower, stripping as he went. The telephone was ringing when he came out. He picked up the receiver.

"Mr. Waller, you have a message. Shall I read it to you?"

"Yes."

"Your ten o'clock appointment has been changed to five o'clock this evening at location number two."

Waller dropped the phone back in its cradle, stretched out on the bed and was instantly asleep.

REGINALD LOOKED up from the account he was posting and saw the boy at the door. He smiled as he joined his nephew on the steps.

"I've sold five dolls so far today," Davy announced proudly. "I want to sell these last three before I quit. Is it okay if I sell in the lobby?"

His mother's words came back to him and Reginald shook his head. "No, you know I can't break the rules, even for you."

A cheeky grin lit the boy's face. "Well, it doesn't hurt to ask."

Reginald ran a fond hand over the boy's head. "Of course, I can't stop you from selling on the street in front of the hotel."

Davy started away then ran back. "Oh, Mama sent you these." He pulled a crumpled pack of Marlboro's from his pocket. "A customer left them on one of her tables. See you later." The boy dashed into the milling throng.

Reginald pulled out two mashed cigarettes, straightened them between his fingers, then slid one back in the pack and put it in his pocket. A quick glance showed there were no guests at the desk requiring service. With a sigh of pleasure, he lit the cigarette and leaned back against the railing watching the street. It was a colorful, crowded scene that always pleased him. Tourists with their cameras, native women and children in their colorful clothes hawking their wares, the small groups of unemployed men crouched against the walls playing dice. His island might be poor but it was alive.

WALLER STOPPED in the door and surveyed the same scene with disgust. He watched a group of tourists dickering with an old woman loaded down with straw hats. His eyes roamed over the street. Nasty white maggots among a swarm of filthy brown roaches and black beetles. He shivered with revulsion. He would have to wade through this sickening mass to keep his appointment with the little cockroach, Castenada. Ignore them, pretend they weren't there. It was the only way. Lifting his head, staring straight ahead, he descended the six steps and started up the street, his gut roiling and skin crawling.

He didn't see the boy who rushed in front of him, a straw doll extended. His stride never slowed as he bumped into Davy, knocking him down. He didn't hear the hollow crunch of bone striking concrete. There was no pause as his left foot flattened the doll nor when his right toe slammed into the boy's temple.

THEY KEPT a silent vigil, clustered around Davy's bed. Not all of his grandmother's powers could save him, at nine the boy died. It was after midnight when they got home from the hospital and the distraught Malia was finally asleep. Reginald sat in the kitchen, elbows propped on the table, head in his hands. A flame of anger burned in the aching hollow in his heart. He wasn't aware of his mother's presence until the old Obeah Woman laid a calloused hand on his shoulder and slid a cup of tea before him.

She sat down across from him. "Tell me what happen. Who do this thing?"

He told her, his voice harsh with anger and grief. His hand beat a tattoo of frustration on the table as he finished. "He didn't even stop, didn't even look down. It was like he'd stepped on a cockroach." He raised his head and looked at her. "Do something, Mama. Use your powers. Make him pay."

HIS MEETING with Castenada successfully completed, Waller strolled back toward the Carib Hotel. Strains of the old song, Lili Marlene, played on steel drums filtered out of a bar. He paused, listening. The song brought back memories of his childhood and of his father and grandfather. He turned towards the door, then hesitated as the music ceased. The band broke into a cacophonous rendition of an old German drinking song and he was drawn inside almost against his will. It had been so long since he had heard it.

A dozen or so tourists, tables pushed together, were grouped in front of the band. Most were swinging their beer mugs in rhythm, some singing drunkenly. Waller selected a shadowed table in the back of the room and ordered a drink.

Hours later he returned to the hotel. He paid no attention to the old woman glaring at him from the shadows. In his room, he stripped and headed for the shower. Water dripping from his wet hair, eyes closed, he stepped out and reached for a towel. At the brittle crunch and slimy feel beneath his foot, his eyes flew open. A cockroach. Bile rose in his throat. He jumped back in the shower stall and turned on the water, frantically scrubbing the sole of his foot.

Drawing the shower curtain aside, he scanned the floor. Bare. He grabbed the towel from the bar. Another roach crawled from its folds and ran across his hand. He yelped and dropped the towel. Trembling, he gently lifted another towel and shook it. No bugs. He rubbed himself dry, wrapped the towel around his waist and opened the bathroom door.

His gaze swept the bedroom. Nothing. With a sigh he crossed the room and slipped on a pair of open sandals. He got a pack of cigarettes out of his suitcase, opened it, removed one and tossed the pack on the dresser. His eyes widened as they caught sight of the juju doll. His breath caught and he backed away. No. No, it wasn't possible. He shook his head, fighting down the rush of fear that threatened to suffocate him.

Superstition. Stupid, ignorant superstition. He said the words aloud and the sound of his voice in the empty room startled him. Of course it was just superstition. They couldn't frighten him. It was nothing but a stupid doll. He started to reach for it, then jerked his hand back. Let the maid get rid of it in the morning.

He took a deep breath and moved out onto the balcony. A cigarette and the night air would calm him. After finishing the cigarette, he stayed for some moments leaning on the rail, enjoying the night, the doll forgotten. A tiny rustle sounded from the room. He stiffened, his muscles on instant alert. He turned slowly.

The bedroom floor undulated with beetles and roaches. His eyes widened in horror. They poured out of the room and onto the balcony in waves, crawling over each other in their rush toward him. Petrified, he could only stare as hundreds, thousands of bugs surged towards his feet.

He screamed and stumbled back against the iron railing. The cockroaches advanced, crawled between his toes, over his arches, up his ankles. He climbed onto the railing, kicking, screaming. The roaches swarmed up the curled metal uprights and onto the top rail, onto his hands, up his arms, across his shoulders. His screams turned into demented shrieks, were choked off....

REGINALD OPENED the door with his passkey, then stepped back to allow the police detective to enter the room. As the detective crossed to the balcony from which the tourist had fallen, Reginald followed him into the room and snatched up the juju doll from the dresser. His hand hesitated over the discarded pack of cigarettes, then he slipped them both into his pocket.

* * * *

The Dark Fuzzies

THE DARK fuzzies had been creeping in all day. Sarah Beth tried to keep them at bay by baking a cake, Tyrone's favorite; a triple layer chocolate with fudge frosting between the layers and a seven minute icing. It hadn't worked. She'd eaten half the cake herself and now the fuzzies were closing in.

She took off the huge apron, a gift from her mother-in-law, picked up her purse and hurried into the garage. Sometimes she could escape the fuzzies by going for a drive.

The garage had become a scary place since the day the fuzzies caught her in the car. That day she'd sat, the motor running, door opener in her hand, trying to decide whether to press the button or not.

Tyrone didn't believe her but she hadn't been thinking of suicide. She just hadn't been able to decide whether or not to open the door. Because once the door was open, she'd have had to decide where to go and it hadn't seemed worth the effort.

She backed the car into the street. Without giving the fuzzies time to confuse her, she headed for State Route 33, away from traffic. The fuzzies were with her, but they seemed content to hover somewhere in the back of the car.

She passed the Grange Hall and a worm of pain gnawed at her insides, just under her heart. Ten years. She'd come to the dance with her cousin, Tammy Lynn. She hadn't wanted to go because she'd known how it would be. The boys all flocked around Tammy Lynn who was so beautiful and knew how to kid around and flirt. Sarah Beth found a seat in the corner content to listen to the music and watch Tammy Lynn.

When Tyrone Chalmers asked her to dance, her mouth went dry and her tongue felt as big as a marshmallow. She could only nod. Tyrone had talked about himself during the whole dance and hadn't seemed to notice her silence.

He'd called on her almost every night for a month. Mostly they sat on the porch swing and he would tell her of his plans. He had plenty of those. He had his life mapped out for the next five years. He was going to be wealthy—maybe not at first, but he'd get there. All he needed was a little capital and a few breaks. Someday he'd be the biggest real estate broker in the state.

Sarah Beth listened, bewildered but fascinated, storing up memories; Tyrone Chalmers was actually sitting on her front porch sharing his dreams with her. Tyrone Chalmers, Lawrenceburg's best quarterback ever, student body president, valedictorian. He'd been the handsomest boy in school; all the cheerleaders had drooled over him. Now he was back, a college graduate and he was actually calling on little Sarah Beth Denny. Sometimes Sarah Beth thought her heart would just swell up and burst from happiness. She was sure it would, the day he told her he was going to marry her. Of course, she hadn't known then that her biggest attraction was the forty acres her Grandaddy Billings had left her. It had given him his start as a real estate developer.

Now, as she drove past the Grange Hall, Beth shook her head trying to escape the memories and to concentrate on the road. She wasn't aware she was crying until she tasted the salty tears that trickled into the corner of her mouth.

TYRONE'S blue Cadillac was parked in the middle of the driveway when she got home. She had to edge two wheels of her vintage Chevy Nova onto the bark of the rose bed to squeeze into the garage. She hoped he wouldn't see the indentations before she had a chance to rake then smooth.

He lowered the newspaper as she entered the room and looked up. "You do remember that I have to attend the school board meeting tonight?"

The fuzzies fluttered at her back. "Yes, dear." She hadn't remembered.

Tyrone dropped the paper and inched back his cuff, exposing his watch and said pointedly, "School board meetings are not dinner meetings."

The fuzzies were all about her as she hurried into the kitchen but kept their distance while she cooked. They never bothered her when she was cooking. It was the only skill Tyrone occasionally praised. And she was a good cook!

They ate at the huge mahogany table in the dining room; the table that had once belonged to some senator. Tyrone had picked up at an estate sale and after that, they didn't eat in the kitchen anymore. Sarah Beth missed the kitchen. After grace, the meal was consumed in silence. Tyrone didn't believe in conversation at the table.

Sarah Beth had been taught from childhood to clean her plate but tonight she had no appetite, pushing the food around on her plate until Tyrone patted his lips with his napkin and stood up.

"Please pack my case tonight. I want to get an early start. I need to be in Nashville by eleven."

Nashville. The name brought a longing so intense it ached. She spoke without thinking. "Can I go with you? I could shop while you're in your meetings. Maybe..." Her heart was racing so that she could hardly speak. "Maybe we could get tickets to the Grand Ole Opry..."

The words died away at the pained expression on his face and she hung her head. "I'm sorry."

The fuzzies came slipping back as she heard the front door slam. Slowly she began stacking the plates and carried them into the kitchen. A steak knife slipped off the stack and landed on the floor. She picked it up. The black fuzzies crowded in, swirling, suffocating her.

"My Lord, girl, what are you doing?"

Sarah Beth looked from the knife in her hand to her neighbor standing in the back door. "Marcia. You startled me."

"Didn't you hear me knock?"

"No. I guess I was day dreaming. Want a cup of coffee?" Interpreting Marcia's glance towards the hall, she smiled. "Tyrone's gone to the school board meeting. Give me a minute to clear the table and we can have a hen party. I baked a chocolate cake this afternoon."

"I'll give you a hand."

When the dishes were done and they were seated at the kitchen table with coffee and cake, Marcia announced, "I'm going to Nashville for the weekend. I've got tickets to the Opry."

Sarah Beth crushed down a surge of envy. "Tyrone's going to Nashville in the morning."

"Hey, that's great. Are you going to the Opry, too?"
"I'm not going."
"Why not?"
"It's a business trip. He's going to be in meeting the whole time."

"So what. You could shop and take in the sights without him. You might even see some of the stars."

Sarah Beth shook her head. "I'd just be in the way."

"Well, I think you should go. I think it's about time you stood up to him. You never go any where."

SARAH BETH lay in bed and stared at the reflection of the street light on the ceiling and listened to Tyrone's snores. Resentment flowed through her. Why couldn't she go to Nashville with him? He rarely took her anywhere. Not that she'd liked being put on display. The few parties he'd taken her to, she'd hated the way everyone had looked at her, especially the men. But when she'd been allowed to slip off to the sidelines, she'd enjoyed watching people. But that had been a long time ago. When was the last time Tyrone had taken her out? Not since they'd lived in Chattanooga. Never since they'd moved back here.

She slid silently out of bed and padded to the bathroom. Under the bright light, she studied her face in the mirror. Her skin was still smooth and youthful except for a few tiny wrinkles around her eyes, the kind her Ma used to call laugh lines. She unbraided her hair and began to brush it. It was the same silvery blond that Tyrone once told her was liquid moonlight and it still fell just below her shoulders. She kept it trimmed to that length because it was what he liked. In the daytime she pinned it in a knot at the back of her head out of her way.

Putting down the brush, she turned and looked in the full length mirror, something she seldom did. Slowly, she unbuttoned the flannel nightgown and let it fall to the floor. The heat of the blood rushing to her head made her slightly dizzy. She could almost hear her mother's shocked voice, "Sinful. Staring at your naked body like a fallen woman. Shame!

Shame!" Sarah Beth had been six at the time.

Now she forced herself to look at her body, at the still firm breasts, the waist that was only slightly bigger than when she had married. Her hips and thighs were more rounded, less boyish. More womanly.

Hastily she struggled back into her nightgown, switched out the light and sat on the edge of the tub. She thought of her cousin, Tammy Lynn, the last time she'd seen her. The trim legs encased in tight jeans, the cotton shirt that barely hid high firm breasts, the concho belt that emphasized a waist as tiny as it was when she was sixteen.

It wasn't fair. Tammy Lynn was twenty-nine, a year older than Sarah Beth. Tyrone didn't even like Tammy Lynn, said she was cheap, a tart. Then why was he always comparing Sarah Beth unfavorably to her cousin? He denied it but it was true. Tears built up behind her closed lids and trickled down her cheeks. In the darkness the black fuzzies closed in, jeering. Sarah Beth plodded back to bed.

"I SHOULD be back Sunday night. If I get held up, I'll call you." He aimed a kiss past her ear, hurried down the steps and into the car. Sarah Beth stood on the porch and watched until his car was out of sight. She knew she should go upstairs and make the bed but she continued to stand, looking down the street. Climbing the stairs seemed too much effort and she sat down in the wicker rocker. The motion was comforting.

She was still rocking two hours later when Marcia mounted the steps. "Hey, Lazy Bones. Taking a day off now that Massa's out of the way?"

Embarrassed, Sarah Beth jumped up. "I was just resting for a moment, enjoying the day."

Marcia cocked her frizzy red head and peered closely into her friend's face. "Honey, you sickening or something? It's going to rain like blazes any minute."

Sarah Beth glanced at the sky and forced a laugh. "I've always loved thunderstorms."

"Well, I don't! How about some coffee. I could use some

cheering up."

Sarah Beth led the way into the house. "You sound like the dark fuzzies got you. What's the matter?"

"Billy just called. His load fell through and he's stuck in Dallas until Monday."

For a moment the statement didn't register. Billy Martin was a long haul trucker and frequently had to lay over for loads. Then she remembered Nashville. "Oh, no. This was your Opry weekend!"

"Yeah. A real bitch, ain't it. Took me five years to talk him into going and six months to get the tickets. The whole weekend was paid for, too; hotel room for tomorrow and Saturday, tickets, even a tour out to Dollywood."

"You could always go by yourself."

Marcia shook her head. "No fun going alone."

"Isn't there someone you can get to go with you? A relative or a friend?"

"Honey, you're the only friend I've got in this town."

They sipped coffee in silence for several minutes. Then Marcia put her cup down and grabbed Sarah Beth's hand. "You come with me! Now stop shaking your head. You know you're dying to go. We'll have a ball, just the two of us."

"I couldn't. Tyrone..."

"We can leave Nashville early Sunday morning and be back before he gets home. He'll never even know unless you tell him."

Sarah Beth's stomach tightened, half in fear, half from excitement. Dare she?

SARAH BETH stared out the window of Marcia's car at the passing countryside with unseeing eyes. Had she really let Marcia talk her into going to Nashville? Tyrone would be furious. It was okay for Marcia to say he'd never find out but Marcia didn't know Tyrone. Should she tell him when he got home or wait for him to bring it up? This was ten times worse than the time she'd gone to the carnival with Tammy Lynn. But if she didn't tell him and he found out...? Anxiety gnawed in her gut. Why had she agreed to come?

But she wanted to...and the Grand Ole Opry...! She'd dreamed of going to Nashville as long as she could remember. Excitement crept in forcing out the anxiety. The lights and music and laughter and fun. Surely he would understand...no, he never understood. Whatever happened, she'd take it because...because he couldn't take it away from her! This weekend was hers and he couldn't take the memories away. Memories weren't something he could shred, like the red dress Tammy Lynn had given her. The resentment she'd felt in the night rushed back. She'd loved that red dress.

SARAH BETH glanced nervously around the dining room as she followed Marcia and the waiter. She felt as out of place as a greased pig at a revival meeting. She was sure to spill something on the white table cloths or knock over the candle and set the whole place on fire. She took the big menu with shaking hands and opened it to hide her face, then gasped when she read the prices. She let Marcia order for both of them and kept her glance pinned to the tablecloth until their food was served. She'd been a fool to come. Tyrone was right, she wasn't cut out for these kinds of places.

"Look. Sarah Beth, look who's here. Right over there. Look."

Marcia's excited whisper brought her head up. She followed Marcia's stare and excitement charged through her like an electric current. She looked at Marcia, wide eyed. "Is it?"

"Yeah. Wow. Can you believe we're just two tables from Clint Black. Do you think he'd give us an autograph? He's looking this way. Sarah Beth, he's looking right as us!"

Marcia's voice had risen to soft squeal.

"Hush, Marcia. He'll hear you." Feeling the hot rush of blood to her face, Sarah Beth turned her head away, her glance flickering over the back of the room. At least no seemed to be paying any attention to them. Her glance shifted over several couples, then focused on a blonde. Tammy Lynn? Here? Her gaze settle on the man across the table from her cousin. She watched her husband pick up her cousin's hand and kiss the fingers.

Then a waiter blocked her view and when he had passed, she saw Tyrone throw several bills on the table and stand up. She watched as he slipped the sequin jacket about Tammy Lynn's shoulders, saw the way his fingers caressed her neck, her hair, flick lightly over her breasts and settle on the curve of her hip as they walked towards the door. Something inside Sarah Beth rose up, choking her, then exploded.

SARAH BETH lay awake most of the night. By morning a curious emptiness had replaced the searing pain. When Marcia noticed her silence at breakfast, Sarah Beth begged off from the tour to Dollywood claiming the rich food of the night before had upset her system. "I think I'll take a nap then do some shopping if I'm feeling better."

As soon as she was alone, Sarah Beth began to put into action the plans she'd made during the long night. First was a call to Uncle Judge in Knoxville. Arlo Hamby had been a superior court judge for over thirty years and all the kids called him "Uncle Judge". Then there was the call to cousin Joe in Laurenceburg. When she'd finished all the calls, she took a taxi to the mall.

"SARAH BETH, I got to admit, you sure had me fooled." Marcia said as she pulled into her driveway. "I thought the dark fuzzies had you bad, but you seem to have shaken them off. You've been like a new person ever since Friday night."

"I think the dark fuzzies just might have found someone else to haunt for a while. Anyway, they won't be bothering me again." She laughed a young, carefree laugh. "Nope, never again."

"You've been acting awful funny. Are you sure you're okay, not coming down with something?"

"I've never felt better in my life!"

"If you say so," Marcia said, her voice tinged with doubt. "I don't think I've ever seen you in anything but print house dresses and that brown suit. You've been spending money like a drunken sailor. Why you must have charged over a thousand dollars worth of clothes on Tyrone's bank card! Maybe cutting off your hair dislocated your brains."

"Don't you like it?"

"Honey, that new style suits you to a T. Between the hair cut and those clothes, you look ten years younger. I just never figured you had it in you to bust loose like this."

"I figured it was time I had some new clothes. Maybe even a new life. A whole new life." She opened the rear door of the car. "Come on, help me put these things in my car."

Arms full of packages, Sarah Beth nudged the car door shut with a designer jeans clad leg. "Just don't expect to drop over for cake and coffee any more. I'm off to Knoxville."

Marcia's moth dropped open. "You're what?"

"Off to Knoxville. Joe and Serena came over yesterday and packed all my things for me and they're already on their way. I'm gonna stay with Uncle Judge and Aunt Molly for a while."

Marcia stopped at the bottom of the front steps and stared up at her friend. "What's Tyrone going to say to all this?"

Sarah Beth shrugged, then grinned impishly. "As Rhett said to Scarlett, 'Frankly, my dear, I don't give a damn.'" She paused on the porch. "There is just one more little thing I want to do before I leave."

Marcia cocked an eyebrow.

"I'm going to bake Tyrone his favorite cake one last time." She was giggling heartily as she reached into the medicine cabinet for the Ex-Lax box.

* * * *

The Revenge of Henry Montrose

HENRY MONTROSE hated computers. He hated Western Seaboard Bank even more than he hated computers.

He slipped the Hank Snow cassette in the tape player and settled back in his chair, letting the music sweep over him. Millicent had loved country music and playing it somehow made her feel closer. He waited patiently for the song that had inspired him, then smiled as he listened to the words.

He stroked the pile of printouts in his lap. It was time to run the test. Sitting up, he turned off the tape player and switched on his IBM computer and the modem. His hands began to tremble, his breathing quickened. He began to type.

Five minutes later he switched off the machines and sat back. There was nothing to do now but wait. Tomorrow, no, today, he would know if his plan, the years of study, the countless hours of hacking would pay off.

Henry stood up, stretched and glanced at the clock. Two A.M., no point in going to bed. He started for the kitchen and a cold beer. In the hall the pain hit, doubling him over. He clutched his upper abdomen and clenched his teeth against the nausea. Dr. Samuels had warned him. But what could the hospital do for him other than keep him sedated? He shuffled into the bathroom and downed two pain pills. When the agony began to ease, he drifted into the living room and sank down in the worn recliner, the only piece of furniture, other than a TV tray, left in the room. Everything else had gone to the Salvation Army.

His eyes sought out the picture on the mantle; a young man in a WWII uniform, his arm around a plump girl. The girl gazed shyly out of the frame at him, her face lit with a happy smile.

Henry lifted a hand in a salute. "Won't be long now, Millie. Just have this one last thing to do." He closed his eyes. Her presence seemed to fill the room. Her laughter echoed in his ears.

She'd been laughing the first time he met her, a soft, joyous ripple that filled him with delight. The sound of her laughter had stayed with him through the landing at Anzio, the mud and rain as he'd slogged through Italy, and later on the push through

France. The memory of her laughter had made the long journey home on the hospital ship bearable. They had been married three days after his discharge. The next day he'd started work as a teller at Market Bank.

His dreams of becoming a mountain climber, of conquering the great mountains of the world had seemed childish once he'd met Millie. He'd settled into work at the bank with the same determination as he'd once challenged mountains. If he couldn't be the best mountaineer, he'd be the best banker. And he had been good. Damned good or he'd never made head bookkeeper. For twenty-nine years, he'd given Market Bank total dedication.

Then Market Bank had been bought out by Western Seaboard and Western Seaboard had installed computers.

Henry stirred restlessly in his chair. Rage gnawed at his belly. Sweat popped out on his forehead. If they had given him a chance, he would have mastered the damned things. But, no, he was too old to learn. That had been their excuse for letting him go. After twenty-nine years, he was out of a job, without a pension, and, worse, without insurance.

His fingers curled like talons on the arm of the chair. He wouldn't have minded for himself, but his Millie, his darling girl, had been the one to suffer. No, there hadn't been much for Millie to laugh about in those last few months before she died.

After ten years, it had still curdled his soul to walk back into Western Seaboard. But it had been necessary. There were still a few employees that remembered him, welcomed him, answered his seemingly innocent questions, been delighted to show off their new systems. He just hoped they wouldn't get in too much trouble.

Henry opened his eyes. Gray daylight flooded the room, picking out the faded red of the worn rug, emphasizing the dust that coated the hardwood floor. Millie had loved the beautiful parquet. Would the new owners install wall to wall carpeting? He found he really didn't care.

He pushed himself to his feet and headed for the bathroom. A cold shower and a pain pill would set him up. He had a lot to do today.

At five minutes past ten o'clock he entered his branch of the

Third National Bank. Although the day was cool, sweat was trickling down his back as he slid a check across the counter. The next few minutes were critical. His knees had about as much strength as wet spaghetti and he had to grip the counter for support. He glanced furtively around. Everything seemed normal. No strangers loitered, no hand descended on his shoulder.

The teller smiled as she asked, "Are you sure you want this in cash? Wouldn't you rather have a cashier's check?"

His throat was tight and dry; he swallowed convulsively. "No. Can you give it to me in hundreds?" The words came out in a hoarse rasp.

"Certainly, Mr. Montrose." She counted out the ten thousand dollars.

With trembling fingers, he tucked the bills into an envelope and stuffed it in his jacket pocket next to his racing heart. It seemed to take hours to cross the lobby but at last he was outside. The air had never smelled so sweet, the sun had never shone so brightly. He'd done it!

A rush of adrenalin made him feel almost young again. He threw back his head and marched down the street. Pain nipped at him but he ignored it. He still had one more piece of business.

Old Margolis, the stone cutter, was surprised at his request but the ten thousand dollars convinced him. Henry knew it would. There wasn't much call these days for Margolis's old world craftsmanship.

Back home, Henry only allowed himself one pain pill. To successfully complete his revenge on Western Seaboard, he'd need a clear head and a steady hand. They would have no trouble tracing the ten thousand dollars to him. He'd planned it that way. What he was going to do now must never be traced.

At precisely eight o'clock that night he turned on the computer and modem and began typing codes and figures from a list of over twenty thousand entries. At 7:32 A.M., Henry shut down, and opening the computer, he removed the innards and stuffed them in a paper bag. Slipping into his coat, he carried the bag down the street and deposited it in a dumpster behind a Radio Shack. Returning to the house, he unhooked the printer and modem and carried them, one by one, out to the trash barrels. By ten o'clock, they'd be on their way to the landfill.

He re-entered the house smiling. It felt good. He couldn't remember the last time he'd smiled. The pain grabbed him, doubling him over, squeezing the breath out of him. Sucking air through his mouth, he waited for the pain to ease. When it did, he shuffled into the bedroom. From the closet, he took out his good suit, white shirt and the tie that had been Millie's last gift. He laid them over the chair, then added the new underwear he'd purchased earlier in the week. He got his good shoes from the closet, ran a cloth over the toes, and placed them on the floor in front of the chair.

In the bathroom, he showered and shaved. He splashed a little Old Spice on his face. Old Spice had always been Millicent's favorite. Would she be able to smell it today?

Dressed in new pajamas, he collected the photograph from the mantle in the living room and placed it on the dresser where he could see it from the bed. He glanced around. Had he forgotten anything? No. It was time.

In the bathroom, he emptied a pill bottle into his hand, filled a glass of water, and began to swallow the pills two at a time. When his hand was empty, he rinsed the glass and replaced it in its holder.

He slid between the sheets in the big bed he'd shared with Millie for so many years. The anger and hate seeped away. *I'm coming, Millie.* He stared at the photograph until his eyes closed.

MADD, GREEN Peace, Mercy Corp and a dozen other charities and organizations found sizable contributions from an anonymous donor in the their accounts. In a small town in Georgia, an elderly widow found a windfall of a hundred and twenty five thousand dollars in her savings account; a young couple in Massachusetts suddenly had the down payment on a house they had never thought to own; in Iowa, a boy's college fund grew, enabling him to complete his education through his doctorate; and so it went throughout the country.

Three months after the death of Henry Montrose, two FBI agents stared at a magnificent marble monument.

"Imagine an older geezer like that stealing ten thousand dollars from Western Seaboard just to buy himself a fancy tombstone."

"I wish we could find the bastard that stole the twenty million dollars from the same bank as easily as we found this guy."

The younger agent leaned over and read the inscriptions aloud.

Millicent Simmons Montrose
born April 16, 1931
died March 30, 1987
"You Light Up My Life"

Henry Alfred Montrose
born September 11, 1925
died March 30, 19—
"The Man Who Robbed The Bank At
Santa Fe And Got Away"

"Hey, do you think he robbed a bank in Santa Fe, too?"

"Nah. That's the title of a country western song. But I suppose we'd better check it out. You never know."

* * * *

Blind Justice

IT WAS RAINING. Light, misty rain. The kind you could walk in all day without really getting wet. The kind of rain for which Seattle was famous. Or infamous.

Although the afternoon was chilly, Billy Joe Corcoran was sweating as he waited behind the wheel of the blue van he'd stolen the night before. Why didn't Fred and Paco come? What was taking so long? He could have robbed half a dozen convenience stores in the time they'd been in the bank.

He heard the muffled crack of Paco's .38 revolver. Panic raced along his nerves like a high voltage electric current. He had to get out of here! There wasn't supposed to be any shooting! His hand gripped the gear lever, but before he could shift, the back doors flew open and his two partners tumbled in, stripping off their masks.

"Get going," Fred yelled as he slammed the doors shut.

Billy Joe didn't have to be told. Before the words were out of Fred's mouth, Billy Joe was pulling away from the curb and racing up the street.

ALBERT FREEMAN walked up the hill to Fourth Street. While he waited for the light to change, he took out his handkerchief and wiped the film of water from the lenses of his horn-rimmed glasses.

There was a squeal of tires behind him as the light changed. Trying to settle his glasses on his nose with one hand while he stuffed the handkerchief away with the other, he stepped off the curb. A instant later he was flying through the air, then sprawling on the wet payment. His glasses, flying from his hand, landed a few inches away. Automatically he reached for them and narrowly missed having his fingers crunched as a booted foot came down on them.

Lying on the wet pavement in stunned surprise, he watched the boots dance a little jig, then a beefy hand collected the broken frames while another hand grasped him under the arm and hauled him to his feet.

"Hey, buddy, are you okay?"

Albert peered myopically into the bearded face. "Yes. Yes, I guess so." He ran an uncertain hand over his face, feeling naked and vulnerable. "My glasses—"

"Sorry. Didn't see them in time. Dammed kids racing around the streets. Got no manners. You sure you're okay?" Keeping a vise-like grip on Albert's arm, he hustled him the rest of the way across the street. "Well, you take care now," the stranger said as they reached the curb.

Albert stared after him for a moment, then looked down at the broken frames in his hand. How was he going to drive home without his glasses? He had a spare pair but a lot of good that did him, now. They were at home in the top right hand drawer of his bureau.

Suddenly conscious of how ridiculous he must look standing in the middle of the sidewalk, he pushed his way through the crowd that had gathered and leaned against the building. Snippets of conversations floated around him, barely impinging on his consciousness, as he rubbed his bruised hip.

"...robbed the bank..."

"...two men in Halloween masks..."

"...shot a guard..."

"I heard they killed three customers..."

Staying close to the buildings, Albert shuffled on shaking legs to the parking garage, took the elevator to the third deck and found his car. He was lucky to be alive, lucky that nothing more than his glasses had been broken. Fumbling with his keys, he bent to peer near-sightedly at the lock, got the door open and climbed behind the wheel of the 1949 Cadillac that had belonged to his father. He ran a hand over the leather upholstery, taking comfort in its rich feel despite its worn, cracked surface. His wife had been after him for years to sell the Cadillac and buy something newer, but the sturdy build and excellent craftsmanship of the old car appealed to him.

He shouldn't drive, but what else could he do? He'd never be able to read a bus schedule without his glasses, he didn't have the money for a taxi, or for that matter, enough to pay for another day's parking. It was hell to be old and broke and...no, he wouldn't get on that track again. Think positive. If he waited until late and stayed on the side streets... The shock of the accident caught up with him and he began to shake. He stretched out on the seat and closed his eyes. He'd rest a while...

BILLY JOE wove through the downtown traffic, avoiding the freeway with its bumper-to-bumper traffic and headed south. Just north of Tukwila, he circled a block, checking to make sure he wasn't being followed, then pulled up to a vacant, ramshackle warehouse. Fred jumped out and opened the door to the right bay, then closed it when Billy Joe drove in.

As Billy Joe walked around the front of the truck, he ran a hand over the left front fender finding only a tiny dent. A nervous giggle erupted from his throat. That old guy had sure looked funny flying through the air.

"Come on, Billy Joe, let's see what we got here," Fred called from the back of the bay. He tossed the gym bag onto an old Formica table while Paco dragged an ice chest from under the table and pulled out three beers. Sipping beer, they counted the money.

Billy Joe giggled again as he stuffed his share into a paper sack. Almost fifteen thousand dollars. It sure beat robbing convenience stores! "Let's go. I wanna get back to California. I hate this rain."

"We wait. Just like we planned. We'll leave at ten, when the traffic has cleared out," Fred snapped. He gestured towards the red Ford Pinto parked in the second bay. "You sure that thing will get us back to L.A.? When I told you to steal something the police wouldn't look at twice, that wasn't exactly what I had in mind."

"Hey, it'll get us there!" Billy Joe said. "I stole it in Oregon, then switched license plates off a wreck in a junk yard in Yakima. I spent three days working on the motor. It purrs like a kitten. And with that new paint job, even the owner wouldn't recognize it. It's the perfect getaway car. Nobody will look twice at an old car like that."

Fred gave the little car another disgusted look and reached for another beer. "Might as well play cards 'til it's time to leave."

WHEN ALBERT Freeman awoke several hours later the parking garage was dark and silent. His head ached and his bruised body protested as he sat up and peered around. Only a few cars remained in the dark and silent garage. He started the motor, and leaning forward over the steering wheel, eyes squinted, he eased down the ramp and into the deserted street. Staying well below the speed limit, he drove south through the empty warehouse area. As he neared Tukwila, his confidence grew. He'd soon be home. Headlights appearing in the rear view mirror distracted him. Cops? Had he been driving too slow?

Then, out of the corner of his eye, he saw a bright red car racing down a side street. Frantically, he hit the brakes, but it was too late. The Cadillac slammed into the side of the red car. He was thrown forward, then jolted sideways, his head banging into the side window. He only had time to be thankful his wife had insisted on installing seat belts before the world spun away into darkness.

Albert was vaguely aware of hands pulling at him. He blinked at the blurred face bending over him. He fumbled in his pocket and pulled out his glasses frames as he was lifted away from the car. The world spun and when it righted itself, he was lying on the pavement in a wash of red and blue lights. Two men in white jackets were bending over him. Beyond the paramedics, he saw several uniformed policemen clustered round the red car. One of them was clutching a gym bag under his arm and three paper sacks in his hands.

Albert struggled to sit up. One of the paramedics gently pushed him down, saying, "Take it easy, Pops. We're going to take you to the hospital for observation, but you're going to be okay. Looks like all you got was a bump on the head and a few bruises."

"What...what happened?"

From somewhere out of the darkness an excited voice exclaimed, "I seen it. I seen it all. Happened right in front of me. Those punks ran a stop sign and you broadsided them.

Man, that old car of yours is a real tank. They sure don't make 'em like that any more! Don't think the frame was damaged. Looks like all it'll need is some body work. You should see that Pinto. Nothing but scrap metal. Those guys were lucky to get out with only a few broken bones."

"My glasses..."

"Sorry, Pops," the paramedic said. "They got broken in the accident."

"But..." Not in the accident, he started to say, then snapped his lips closed. If he had admitted he'd been driving without them, they might take away his license, might even take him to jail, blame the accident on him. Better to say nothing.

Bright lights blinded him and he put up his hand to shield his eyes. Somewhere a woman's voice was saying something about a bank robbery.

"What'd you say, Pops?" the paramedic asked.

"Nothing. Just...I...I can't see without them."

Suddenly a pretty blonde woman was leaning over him holding a microphone in front of his face. He tried without success to shove it away. The lights were making his head ache. The woman was saying, "This man is the hero of the hour. Tell me, how does it feel to have foiled the bank robbers' getaway? Did you know they shot and killed a guard at the bank this afternoon? Did you know the bank was offering a reward for their capture?"

He closed his eyes wishing everyone would go away.

"How about that, Pops," the paramedic said. "You'll be able to buy a dozen pairs of glasses."

* * * *

Trick or Treat

ABIGAIL FOSTER sat at the kitchen table pleating and unpleating a handkerchief that had belonged to her mother. The ticking of the clock on the wall echoed through the room, drawing her unwilling glance. Three-thirty.

Memories crowded in. Mama at the sewing machine making her a princess costume, and once, a real tutu. Daddy holding her hand to cross the street then waiting on the sidewalk while she rang door bells. Halloween had been her favorite holiday, after Christmas, of course. Later, there were Halloween dances at the high school. Three years in a row she had won the prize for best costume. Halloween had been fun back then.

Not that they had been angels, oh, no, far from it. Her lips curled into a smile as she remembered the time they had taken apart Mr. Johanson's farm wagon and the boys had hoisted in onto the church roof and put in back together. That year Halloween had fallen on Saturday. It had taken them all night. She'd been so sleepy the next morning she'd almost missed church. Abigail chuckled aloud. The expression on everyone's face when they'd arrived for services!

Her smile died away. They had played tricks back then but they hadn't been destructive. The boys had brought the wagon down and put it back together for Mr. Johanson. In fact, they had greased it and even replaced some of the rusted bolts and cracked sideboards. When they had soaped windows or other mischievous things, they'd always gone back the next day and washed the windows and cleaned up any mess.

But now....

Her glance skittered back to the clock and hastily away. Four o'clock. The little ones would be coming soon. At least she could enjoy them. It was a shame so many mothers no longer took the time or made the effort to create costumes. Now most of the children wore those cheap things from the dime store, if they wore any at all. Abigail felt sorry for them. Costumes had been more than half the fun of Halloween. Oh, well, new times, new ways. They probably didn't know what they were missing.

Heaving to her feet and ignoring the pain in her knee, she

shuffled to the counter and picked up the tray of sugar cookies cut in shapes of pumpkins, cats and witches. She felt a twinge of embarrassment at the crooked faces and lopsided grins. The arthritis that deformed her fingers made squeezing the icing cone difficult. But the little ones wouldn't mind. They never did. Some of them were even polite and thanked her.

The doorbell rang before she was half way down the hall. Icy fingers raced up her spine. The night had begun.

By seven, dusk had given way to full dark. She switched off the front porch light and carried the half dozen remaining cookies into the kitchen. The others would be coming soon. It was time to soak the rug.

Hobbling onto the back porch she pressed the jury-rigged switch. From the shed behind the garage, the powerful industrial generator roared to life. She waited, listening, until it settled into a steady growl.

It didn't take her long to complete her preparations. She'd had a year to make her plans. It had taken her almost that long, because the dexterity had long left her fingers, and pain had made the physical labor difficult. She shuffled back to the living room, turning off lights as she went. Just inside the living room arch, she stopped to tuck a cord out of sight, to smooth and adjust the big, sopping wet, oriental rug that covered the sheet of steel.

Wait! The new cell phone! Where had she put it? For a moment panic raced through her. She crossed the room and ran her fingers over the table. Yes, it was there.

In the dark, she settled into the big chair that had been her husband's and waited. Perhaps they wouldn't come. Please, Lord, don't let them come this year.

The chair, molded to Michael's big frame, seemed to enfold her, comforting her. She could almost feel her husband's arms cradling her. His voice, hoarse and gasping, echoed in her ears. *Take care of yourself, darling girl. I'll be waiting.*

The bigger children came and went. She knew she'd find her yard filled with trash in the morning but she didn't really mind. It was harmless fun and young Robert from down the street would clean it up. He could always use an extra five dollars. Such a nice young man. Not like the others.

She heard them. Over the blaring music she could hear the shouted obscenities, the raucous laughter. Turning her head, she glanced out the window. They were across the street, at the Crawford's. Tears welled up and ran down her cheeks. Poor Betsy must be terrified, confined to her hospital bed, completely helpless. Henry hadn't been able to protect her last year and he wouldn't be able to this year. No eighty-seven year old man could stand up to that bunch of rowdies and he'd become so frail.

She reached for the phone, her fingers fumbling as punched 911. Her hands were shaking so hard she dropped the phone. She heard it bounce and skitter away on the hardwood floor.

Maybe they would go away. Maybe the police would come in time this year. Please, God. Oh, God! They were in the Crawford house. Pain tore through her. Was that Betsy she heard screaming or was it just in her mind? She clamped her hands over her ears and shut her eyes, her lips moving in silent prayer.

The noise they called music surged louder and Abigail opened her eyes. They were outside. Panic flooded through her. They were crossing the street. Coming up her walk.

Her trembling fingers flew to the switch on the side table and sent it sliding across the polished wood. Panic raced through her, followed by a sharp pain in her chest. Gasping, she lunged sideways, grasping the switch before it could fall and clutched it in her lap.

The pounding on the door made her jump and she swallowed convulsively. Go away! Go away! It was a silent scream. The glass in the front door shattered sending shards of terror through her. Her breath came in short, painful gasps.

"Trick or treat," a voice yelled. A course laugh followed.

The door crashed open. Heavy feet crunched through the broken glass and pounded down the hall. The blaring music hammered in her head until she thought it would burst. Her very bones seemed to melt like Jell-O on a hot day, she felt herself shriveling, the room dissolving. It was going to happen again. She mustn't faint. Oh, God, please don't let me faint. Not now,

God. Not now!

"Hey, old lady. We gotta Halloween treat for you. Come on out and see what we got for you. It's nice and long and hard."

He was in the archway. His silhouette seemed to grow before her eyes until it filled the doorway. From somewhere behind him, she heard the girl's voice. "Turn on some fucking lights."

Abigail shivered and clamped her lips over the scream that was tearing at her throat. She'd screamed last year, screamed and begged, but it hadn't stopped them. The girls had been the worst. What the boys had done...that most terrible thing...But the girls...the girls had been even worse. They'd watched. Watched and sniggered and made such cruel remarks. And afterward it had been one of the girls who had smashed her kneecap.

They crowded into the room. Six of them. The same as last year. Abigail's body began to tremble. The pain in her chest intensified, radiating into her arms, making breathing difficult. She had to end it. End it now. She reached up and turned on the table lamp.

"Hey. Been waiting for us?"

Incredible. She realized she was shaking her head in disbelief. His clean cut, almost innocent look under that weird spiky hair had fooled her last year. Not now. Her gaze followed his hand as he reached down and unzipped his pants.

"Trick or treat."

Her glance flew back to his grinning face. Her lips felt as dry and stiff as beef jerky. Her words came out cracked and harsh. "Yes. Trick or treat."

She flipped the switch.

ABIGAIL WAS still sitting in the chair absently watching the play of the flashing blue and red lights over the trees and shrubbery when the men crossed the street. She knew she should get up and go to the door but the pain in her chest kept her pinned to the chair.

She heard their voices in the hall. "In here," she called. The effort of those two words seemed to drain the last of the strength from her body and she slumped down in the chair. From somewhere out of the darkness, she thought she heard her mother saying, "Ladies never slouch," and she struggled to sit up straight.

Then other voices, men's voices, penetrated the fog that was rapidly surrounding her.

"Dead. Every damned one of them is dead. Not a mark on them."

"Look at their shoes."

"Melted? Jesus! They've been electrocuted."

"Hey, what's this under the rug? What's this doing here? These wires—"

"Get back! They may still be hot! Call in and have them send out an electrician."

She wanted to reassure them, to tell them she'd turned off the switch but it was too much effort. The terrible pain in her chest was easing, draining the last of her strength with it. She saw her husband standing in the shadows, waiting. *I did it, Michael. I took care of myself.* He nodded and held out a hand to her.

The voices intruded and she looked back at the policemen clustered in the doorway.

"If this is the same gang that attacked her last year, I'd say they got what they deserved."

"You think that old lady did this? Look at her. She must be a hundred years old."

"Ninety-three," she whispered.

"Hey, lady, hang in there. We got an ambulance coming."

"How the hell could an old woman like that dream this up?"

Abigail wanted to say, "My husband was a master electrician. He always said I was his best apprentice," but she didn't have the strength. Besides, Michael was waiting and she was ready to go. She smiled.

* * * *

Threadneedle on the Loose

A Simon Threadneedle Mystery

Prologue

SIMON Threadneedle knew he should be happy. Well, maybe not happy, but at least satisfied. They'd finally caught the slimeball that had raped and murdered three young boys. It had been a good bust, everything done right, all of *i's* dotted and *t's* crossed. The evidence he and his partner, Brian Cully, had collected should put the creep away for the rest of his life, even if the D.A. didn't go for the death penalty.

What he really needed was a cold six-pack to unwind. He sighed aloud, remembering that he'd drank the last can the night before. Oh, well, he'd stop at the liquor store up the street.

He pulled into the curb and heaved his tired body out of the car. It had been a hell of a long day, a long week. TGIF. He crossed the sidewalk and pushed open the door, and stopped, the hairs on the back of neck rising up like soldiers on parade.

"Oh, shit!"

He threw himself sideways, reaching for gun at his back. Even as his fingers locked around the butt and dragged it from its holster, he felt the first bullet slam into him.

On his back, Threadneedle raised the gun, centered it on the punk's chest and squeezed the trigger. A neat, red hole appeared in the kid's chest as he fell backwards, his gun spraying a line of holes up the front window and into the ceiling.

A woman's screams followed Threadneedle as he crawled behind a rack of magazines. More shots erupted, shredding the paper over his head. Footsteps pounded toward him, then the second hold-up artist was in front of him, his machine pistol flashing. Another blow struck Simon as he squeezed off another round. The kid staggered out the door.

Threadneedle knew he'd been hit and wondered why he didn't feel anything. Then the pain washed over him and the room began to fade away.

Someone was bending over him. He tried to speak but couldn't seem to form the words or understand what the man in white was saying. Someone was ripping away his shirt and it hurt like hell. He drifted into darkness and before everything went black he saw the faces of the punks clearly. Neither could have been over twelve years old.

Then he got the words out. "Damned kids ought to be in school."

Chapter 1

THE SALESMAN glanced from the check on the counter to Simon, a frown creasing his forehead and suspicion obvious in his narrowed eyes. Simon sighed inwardly as he slipped his drivers license and the card that identified him as a detective sergeant with the Los Angeles Police Department, the word "Retired" stamped across it, from his wallet and dropped them on the counter. It was something he'd had to put up with all his life.

With a name like Simon Threadneedle, most people seemed to expect him to be a mousy little man, inoffensive, dapper, with probably an Adolph Menjou moustache. A tailor or maybe an accountant. Certainly not an ex-wrestler, ex-Delta Force officer, and now ex-policeman.

At fifty-nine, Simon stood six-feet-six with a chest that measured fifty-two inches, brawny arms, legs as large as tree trunks and a lantern jaw. He weighed the same as he had in college, two hundred seventy pounds, and not an ounce of it was fat. He'd kept himself in shape by working out daily and eating sensibly. He still had a full head of dark brown hair with only a touch of gray at the temples.

The clerk shoved the two pieces of identification back across the counter with a weak smile and quickly bagged the fishing lures, reel, Finnish filleting knife and other gear and taped the sales slip to the spinning rod. "Have a good day," he called as Simon walked away with his purchases.

Right. Have a good day. Bullshit. He hadn't had a good day in nearly a year, not since he'd walked into an armed robbery in progress at his neighborhood liquor store and taken three bullets from two punks that should have still been playing with Tonka Toys. The bullet wounds to his thigh, stomach and shoulder had healed, but the powers-that-be had decided to stick him with a desk job when he'd returned to work. More bullshit. After twenty-five years on the force he'd opted for retirement.

He tossed the gear on the front seat and climbed into the cab of his new Chevy three-quarter-ton, four-wheel-drive pickup. The only thing good about today was that it was his last day in this frigging town.

He made four more stops. First to have a canopy fitted on the back of the truck, then to have a trailer hitch mounted, then to pick up the new 26 foot Travel-Eze trailer, and finally to have the two propane tanks filled.

He backed the trailer into the driveway of the bungalow he'd rented for the last ten years. He felt no regret at leaving the place. It had never been home. Home was the big house he'd bought when he and Hannah had first married, where they'd raised their two children. But Hannah had been killed in a traffic accident and once both kids were away at college, he'd taken advantage of the soaring real estate market to sell the house and invest the proceeds.

He climbed out of the cab, unlocked the trailer, and then entered the house. Except for a few cartons piled by the front door, the house was empty. Last month the kids, Anna Marie and Orin, had visited to select whatever furniture and keepsakes they'd wanted. Yesterday the Salvation Army had come to pick up the rest of the stuff, and without a bed, he'd spent last night in a motel. Tonight he'd sleep in the trailer.

He began carrying the cartons out to the trailer. In the morning he'd be on his way. For the next few years he planned to fulfill a life long dream. He was going to really see the United States.

His retirement check was deposited directly into his checking account. He'd arranged with his bank for the automatic transfer of funds from savings to checking if he was ever overdrawn. For the first time in his life, he carried credit cards: two bank cards, two gasoline company cards and an ATM card with which he could access his checking account from anywhere in the country.

Borrowing a neighbor's hose, he filled the water storage compartment of the trailer. When he had his possessions arranged in the trailer to his satisfaction, he went back to the house for one last walk-through and locked the door.

In the last dim light of day, he sat at the dinette in the trailer and addressed an envelope to the rental agency, enclosed the house key, sealed and stamped the envelope. In the morning, he'd drop it in a mailbox on his way out of town.

Undressing in the dark, he crawled into bed. Tomorrow he'd be on his way. He'd go where he wanted, when he wanted, stopping when and where he felt like it. No schedules, no itinerary. Footloose. Footloose and fancy free. He fell asleep with a wide smile on his face.

SIMON YAWNED a mighty yawn and blinked his eyes, trying to focus on the narrow, winding two-lane road. Since he'd left Los Angeles he'd gotten into the habit of taking afternoon naps. Now he had trouble staying awake after lunch; although he hadn't eaten since morning, drowsiness was creeping up on him.

In the last month he'd traveled only a little over seven hundred miles, stopping frequently, often for days at a time. He'd toured William Randolph Hearst's monument to his ego, stopped for a couple of days at Big Sur, explored the Monterrey Peninsula and caught a brief glimpse of Clint Eastwood in Carmel. He'd visited Fisherman's Wharf—a disappointment—rode the cable cars—enjoyable but crowded—and other tourist attractions in San Francisco where he'd spent a week. He'd spent a couple of days in the wine country sampling its products and camped for days in the redwoods, thrilled by their majesty.

He'd left California behind early this morning and had been enjoying the Oregon coast until his newly acquired penchant for afternoon naps began to interfere. He rubbed the week-old stubble on his face with a vigorous hand trying to chase away the lethargy.

His fingers played with the growth on his chin. After years of being clean-shaven he'd decided to grow a beard. The idea of never having to shave again appealed to him, another benefit of being on the loose for the first time in his life, but the damned thing itched like crazy. He supposed he'd get used to it in time and he'd been told the itching would stop as it grew out.

He rounded a curve and slammed on the brakes. He swerved, barely missing the battered pickup with a homemade wooden camper on the back. It blocked half the traffic lane. The sudden rush of adrenaline had him wide-awake by the time he'd pulled to a stop ahead of the other vehicle.

He jumped out of the cab and charged back to the obviously disabled vehicle. A pair of legs clad in worn and dirty jeans dangled over the left front fender; the upper body bent over the motor. The feet, which dangled a good six inches off the ground, were shod in cracked boots with holes in the soles.

"Damn it, man, why don't you have flares out? You're blocking half the road."

From under the hood a gravelly voice said, "Ain't got any."

Simon turned and hurried back to his pickup, collected half a dozen flares from his own supply and jogged around the curve, setting three of them at the approved distance to warn approaching vehicles. He retraced his steps and placed the other three to flag oncoming traffic.

When he returned, he found the other driver perched on the fender rolling a cigarette, a battered Stetson pulled low over his forehead. He didn't look up until he had the cigarette lit. Then Simon found himself looking into a pair of faded blue eyes that glinted with humor. They were set in a weathered and lined face the color and texture of old leather.

"I thankee, son."

Simon's anger drained away as he studied the old man. He was skinny as the proverbial rail, his grey hair pulled back into a scraggly ponytail and held in place by a rubber band. His shirt was as faded as his jeans but had been neatly mended.

"What seems to be the problem?"

"Water pump."

Simon glanced around. The shoulder of the road was too narrow to get the truck completely off the pavement and was bordered by a deep drainage ditch. "I could take you into the nearest town but it wouldn't be safe to leave your truck parked like that."

The old man hopped off the fender. "They's a pullout up around the bend, not over a quarter of a mile." He looked at

Simon's rig and frowned. "Don't reckon there's any way you could give me a tow."

Simon studied the rear of his trailer. "Is the road level?"

"Yep."

Simon glanced at the pickup. "You got a tow strap?"

"Yep, but it ain't long enough."

"I've got one. I think if we tied them together it might work. How are your brakes? I don't want the back end of my trailer smashed in."

"Brakes on old Lucy here are just fine." The old man patted the rust-streaked fender.

For all his age, he was spry as a monkey, shimmying under the trailer to fasten one end of the strap to the axle, then scampering back to do the same to his truck.

Simon threw his truck in low gear and eased up the road, praying they wouldn't meet a logging truck or a State Patrol cruiser. When both vehicles were safely parked at the scenic overlook, they trotted back to collect the flares and deposited them on the gravel to burn out.

Simon unhitched his trailer and blocked the wheels while the old man undid the tow straps. As he handed the strap to Simon, the old man said, "You needn't have done that."

"I'll take you into the next town. It's Lion Rock, isn't it?"

"Yep, but the thing is, I'm a mite short of cash right now."

"You live in that camper?"

"Sure do. She's a honey, ain't she? I built her myself."

Simon walked back and studied the camper. To him, it was an ungainly monstrosity but there was no question that the workmanship was flawless. While he examined it, his mind was working. He really couldn't leave the old man out here. It wasn't even a rest area. There was probably a law against parking here more than a few hours. If the truck got towed away, the old man would lose his home and be stuck with towing fees and impound charges. Short of cash, hell. The old man probably didn't have more than a couple of bucks in his pocket. How much did a water pump cost? A couple of hundred dollars? Maybe he was a sucker, but what the hell, he could afford it. Call it his good deed for the day. Make that...year.

He shrugged and walked to his truck. "Come on, old timer. I'll stake you to a water pump."

As they started down the road, the old man stuck out a grubby hand. "Name's Wheatly...Horace Wheatly. Most folks just call me Wheat."

Simon reached across to shake the calloused hand. "Simon Threadneedle."

The pungent odor of the tide flats tickled Simon's nose long before he drove over the bridge that crossed a small river flowing down from the mountains. Several dilapidated piers thrust out into the river and the half a dozen long sheds crowding along the waterfront appeared abandoned.

Lion Rock wasn't much of a town. The business district stretched along the highway for about three blocks. Houses clung to the side of the hill above the highway and below the road were a couple of motels looking across a strip of beach to a minuscule bay. Out in the bay Simon saw a jumble of rocks. As he watched, the rocks seem to undulate.

Wheat followed Simon's startled stare and chuckled. "Sea lions."

Of course. Simon pulled his gaze back to the road and concentrated on his driving.

"They's a NAPA store 'tother end of town," Wheat said as Simon cruised slowly down the highway.

They passed Jack's Market, which reminded Simon that he was running low on coffee and bread and when they passed the Seaside Cafe, his stomach grumbled.

Simon found the auto parts store and purchased the water pump. Heading back out of town they stopped at the market and he picked up groceries, including a half rack of beer. Changing the water pump was likely to be a thirsty job.

A car with Ohio plates pulled out from in front of the Seaside Cafe and without thinking twice, Simon swung in to the curb.

"I'm hungry. Let's grab a bite before we go to work."

"Guess I could use a cuppa coffee."

The Cafe was small with only a half a dozen tables in front of the windows and a dozen stools at the counter. Husky men dressed in heavy trousers cut off six inches or so above the tops of sturdy boots and held up by suspenders occupied three of the stools. Loggers. They were the only patrons. Obviously the lunch rush, if there was one, was over.

Selecting the second table, Simon settled into a chair and reached for the hand written menu. He'd hardly had time to glance at it when a glass of water was slammed down in front of him.

He looked up at the waitress who was glaring at Wheat with dislike. "You figuring to eat today or just take up space?"

"Now, Ruthie, that ain't no way to talk to a customer."

"Hah!"

"Simon, this here is Ruthie. She owns the place and she ain't near as mean as she sounds." He grinned up at the woman. "And she makes the best apple pie you ever sunk your teeth into."

"You ain't getting a free piece today so you might as well save your smooth talking." She eyed Simon. "You planning to eat?"

"Give us a couple of the deluxe cheeseburgers, fries, and coffee. A couple of slices of that apple pie, too."

"Huh! Big spender, are you?"

While they waited for their food, Wheat asked Simon where he was headed.

"My son lives in Seattle. I plan to visit him for a while. Just taking my time and seeing something of the country on my way north."

When their food came they ate in silence. Wheatly ate with the concentration of a hungry man and Simon wondered how long it had been since the old man had last eaten.

On the drive back, Wheat chuckled and nudged Simon in the ribs. "So what do you think of Ruthie? She's something, ain't she?"

The sun was low on the horizon by the time they had the new water pump installed and the radiator filled. Wheat helped Simon hitch the trailer, then leaned against the side and rolled a cigarette. "You planning to drive on?"

"Only as far as the nearest trailer park."

"That'd be on up the road about thirty miles. I hear they charge you an arm and a leg. Why don't you follow me. We got room at our camp and it won't cost you nothin'."

"How far is it?"

"Just a few miles."

Simon hesitated, then shrugged. He liked Wheat and this was beautiful country. If there was a charter boat, he might go deep-sea fishing. If not, he could try his hand a surf casting or fishing the river they'd crossed. "Why not? Lead on out."

Dark clouds rolled in from the ocean as they drove back through Lion Rock. As they turned inland on a gravel road, it began to drizzle. The road wound through dense forest and began to climb. Simon was having second thoughts even before Wheatley turned off on an old logging road. If there had been a spot wide enough to turn his rig around, he'd have headed back to the highway. As it was, he had no choice but to continue.

He gritted his teeth and cussed Wheatly under his breath as the road deteriorated into two barely discernable tracks and the undergrowth scraped the sides and undercarriage of his truck.

Suddenly Wheatly's brake lights came on, casting an eerie red glow over the encroaching wilderness. Simon heard Wheatly's door slam and fumbled under his seat for the Glock 40 caliber automatic he'd carried for last few years. Placing it out of sight along his right leg, he waited and watched, seeing little through the heavily falling rain.

After what seemed an eternity, he heard Wheatly's door slam again and the truck crept slowly ahead then angled off to the left. Simon followed, inching his way through the break in the undergrowth. After perhaps fifty feet, Wheatly stopped again.

Simon felt for, and found, the gun as the old man appeared along side the truck. He grinned as he flipped a wave at Simon and walked back the way they'd come.

Simon shut off his motor and cracked his window half an inch. From somewhere behind he heard strange noises, as though something or someone was thrashing through the brush. The hairs on the back of Simon's neck began to dance the Watusi and his fingers tightened on the gun. He couldn't believe he'd been such a fool as to be suckered in by the old man.

He caught a glimpse of movement out of the corner of his right eye and swiveled his head in time to see Wheatly disappearing into the dark along side the camper. A moment later he heard the truck door slam again and the pickup began to inch forward.

Reluctantly Simon followed. He had no choice unless he wanted to sit where he was until daylight. There seemed to be no break in the dense forest around him. From what little Simon could see, they weren't on a road and even the old trail they had been following had disappeared.

He cussed himself for a fool. After twenty-five years on the Los Angeles Police Force, twelve of them as a homicide detective, he'd let himself be gulled by an old man. Well, if they planned to rob and kill him, they were in for a big surprise. The Glock carried a fourteen round clip and one in the chamber. Fifteen shots. He had two more clips under the seat. They'd find out they'd bitten off more than they'd bargained for.

Wheatly's truck suddenly slewed to the left. Simon slammed on his brakes. Brightly illuminated in his headlights stood a man dressed in army fatigues, feet apart and planted firmly in front of Simon's bumper. Cradled in his arms was an AK-47.

Chapter 2

HEART POUNDING, Simon hit the brakes, slammed the truck into park and waited. Adrenalin raced through his system. The Glock was no match for the automatic weapon. What the hell had he gotten himself into? Simon stared at the man who stared back with cold, blank eyes. He thought he saw movement in the darkness, but before he could turn his head, Wheatly's grinning face appeared at the left window.

"Come on out and meet everybody," the old man said.

Simon continued to stare at the AK-47. Wheatly followed his gaze and grimaced, then yelled, "Andy, put that danged thing up. This here's a friend of mine."

When Andy continued to stare at Simon, Wheatly raised his voice. "Damn it, Andy, stop it. You're scaring my friend."

Andy shook himself, much like a dog shaking off water, and blinked. His posture relaxed slightly and he looked at Wheatly. Then he nodded, turned and ambled off into the darkness.

Simon could feel the sweat trickling down his spine. He couldn't remember being quite so scared for a long, long time.

Wheatly turned back to Simon, the grin back on his face. "That's just Andy. Don't pay him no mind. He ain't dangerous; it's just that sometimes he thinks he's back in Nam. Come on out and meet everybody."

As Simon hesitated, his heart still pounding uncomfortably, a young woman came out of the darkness and shyly approached. She sent Simon a swift, uneasy glance and looked hopefully at Wheatly. "Did you bring the bread?" Her voice was soft and pleasant.

"Gosh, Meg, I plumb forgot."

The woman's face fell. She started to turn away but Wheatly stopped her. "Meg, I'd like you to meet a friend of mine. This here's Simon Threadneedle. He's from Californy.

Meg and her daughter, Jamie, are staying with us for a while."

Meg cast him a quick glance, then stared at the ground as she said, "I'm pleased to meet you. If you'll excuse me, I got to see to Jamie."

"I've some bread in the trailer," Simon said, then wished he'd kept his mouth shut. Getting the bread meant getting out of the truck and he wasn't sure he wanted to.

Meg's face lit up, a wide smile spreading across her face. "Oh, thank you. Jamie's tired of eating peanut butter from the jar."

With a sigh of resignation, Simon turned off the lights and the motor. The darkness was complete. Surreptitiously he pulled out his shirttail, slid the gun into his waistband and covered it with his shirttail, then reached in the glove box for his flashlight. He opened the door and stepped out and was immediately drenched. He made a quick dash for the trailer, fumbled the door open and hopped inside.

Meg and Wheatly had followed him in. Meg was looking around the trailer with wide, admiring eyes. He quickly found a half a loaf of bread and extended it toward her. She hesitated, saying, "Oh, I couldn't take it all."

"Go ahead. I've got another loaf and I can always get more."

She glanced at Wheatly then back at Simon. "Thanks," she whispered. Clutching the bread to her chest, she dashed out the door. Simon stared after her.

"You might as well leave your rig right here for tonight. Ain't nobody coming or going. Tomorrow you can get 'er turned around and I'll introduce you to everybody."

"How many of you are there?"

"Well, now, let's see. There's Meg and Jamie and you saw Andy. Then there's Lovey Coltrane, Buford, Billy Joe and Frannie and George. With me, I guess that makes nine." He backed out the door. "See you in the morning."

He disappeared into the darkness leaving Simon staring after him. Simon stood in the door staring out into the night until the cold rain drove him back. Just where in the hell was he and what kind of mess had he gotten himself into? Wherever it was, he was stuck here until morning. Even if he could get his rig backed around, there was no way he could find his way down the mountain road in the dark.

With a shrug, he opened the door and stepped out into the rain, dashed to the truck and locked it, stopped to turn on the propane and hurried back inside, locking the door after him. He was soaked to the skin and shivering with cold. He lit the propane light, then the heater and stripped off his wet clothes, dumping them in the tiny shower stall. After toweling himself dry, he dug out pajamas and a robe and started a pot of coffee. While it was brewing, he dried, cleaned and oiled his gun. If they thought to attack him while he slept they would be in for a big surprise. He poured himself a mug of coffee, and with the gun beside him, he settled back on the bench seat of the dinette to wait out the night.

A VIOLENT pounding on the side of the trailer awakened him. He struggled out of his cramped position on the seat and rubbed his aching neck as he crossed to the door. Before he could open it, Wheatly's voice boomed, "Hey, Simon, you awake? Simon?"

Simon lowered the top half of the window and blinked at the brightness. "I'm awake, now."

"Well, come on out and meet everybody."

"Let me get some clothes on."

"Okay, but hurry up."

Simon washed the sleep out of his eyes and studied himself in the mirror. He looked like hell and felt worse. His back ached and his neck still had a crick in it from falling asleep at the dinette. He was too old for this! At least the beard he was trying to grow had stopped itching. Not that it was really a beard, yet, just an inch or so of scraggly whiskers. Maybe he should give up and shave. He shook his head. No, he'd give it another week.

He dug out a pair of jeans and a sweatshirt. In the kitchen, he hesitated, then tucked the gun in his waistband, pulling the bottom of the sweatshirt to hide it. He still didn't know what he'd gotten himself into and there was no point in taking chances.

Wheatly was waiting for him as stepped out of the trailer. In daylight, he could see that he was parked in the middle of a small clearing surrounded by thick forest. The pounding rain of the night had passed but the air was still heavily laden with moisture. Fingers of mist swirled at ground level. Above, the giant trees formed a canopy shading the filtered light with a pale green cast that was repeated in the moss that covered their trunks and was repeated again in the giant ferns that grew between the trees. He could almost imagine that he had stepped into some magical undersea world.

He breathed deeply, taking in the scent of pine and moist earth. The damp air made him cough, bringing up phlegm that tasted of smog. When the spasm passed, he took another look around.

Wheatly had moved his truck and Simon saw an old Buick station wagon parked under the trees with a piece of plastic canvas rigged out from the back. A folding table and a couple of lawn chairs were arranged under the canvas.

Beyond the Buick, an eight by ten tent had been pitched. An older Chevy pickup with a camper shell parked beside it. His rig blocked his view of the rest of the clearing.

"Come and meet everyone. You can park your rig later. Andy and George have cleared out a space for you."

Simon followed the old man around the front of his truck and stopped. The clearing was not as big as he'd first thought. A few feet ahead of his front bumper was a fire ring encircled by several stumps on which sat a motley assortment of humans. Beyond the fire was a beat-up, rusted pickup with Kentucky plates and a two-man pup tent. Farther to his right was a very small trailer and a '49 Ford coupe and beyond that stood an old and rusted Plymouth Fury.

"Come on. Everybody's anxious to meet you. I done told them how you helped me."

Simon studied the group with dismay as he walked toward them. A pair of aging hippies, a punk with long hair, a bum with a scraggly beard, the freaked-out survivalist and the young woman he'd seen the night before. What a conglomeration of misfits. Still, they seemed harmless enough. Even Andy seemed less threatening in the daylight. At least there was no sign of the

AK-47.

Wheatly followed Simon's gaze and said, "Andy Mason. Don't let him worry you; he's okay. Ain't you, Andy?"

Andy nodded and continued to study Simon with sharp eyes.

Wheatly continued, "You met Meg last night. This here's her daughter, Jamie." He indicated the child playing in the mud. The little girl, intent on the designs she was drawing in the mud, didn't look up. Simon guessed her to be about five.

"Frannie and George Paulus," Wheatly continued, indicating the pair of aging hippies, "And the fellow with the gee-tar is Billy Joe Johnson. And this here's Buford. Lovey ain't up yet so I'll have to introduce you to her later. Come see where we fixed you a place for your trailer."

"Uh, I was thinking I probably ought to head on out this morning."

"Well, now, I don't reckon that's such a good idea."

Simon stiffened, suddenly glad of the gun in his belt. "Why not?" he asked in a cold voice.

"Well now, they's a couple of reasons. First off, with all the rain we had last night, I've a doubt you could make it down the mountain in the rig of yours without getting stuck."

Wheat grinned, showing a mouth full of snaggled and stained teeth. "Then I figure I owe you for what you did for me. I like to pay my debts."

He walked a few more feet and pointed to where the thick underbrush had been cleared away between two trees and an attempt made to level the ground.

"That big enough for your rig?" Without waiting for an answer, he went on, "I seen the way you got your gear just throwed in the back of your truck. Now I ain't got no money to repay you, but I do got some fine oak I sort of...liberated...awhile back. I figure to build you a nice storage compartment. It'll take me a couple of days to do it right. By that time the road should be dried out enough. Me or Billy Joe will guide you down to the highway."

He stopped and looked up at Simon. "Fair enough?"

"Fair enough."

Wheatly grinned. "Good. As soon as the ground dries out a little, we can dig you a septic pit for your trailer. In the meantime, there's a one-holer over there in the woods." He turned away, then turned back. The grin was gone and his eyes were steely. "We may be poor, but we're all honest folks here. You won't be needing that gun."

They locked glances and Simon's eyes fell first. "No. No, I don't suppose I will."

With Billy Joe and George guiding him, he backed the trailer into the cleared space. His stomach was growling, reminding him that he'd had nothing to eat since the afternoon before and he was craving a cup of coffee. As soon as they had the trailer blocked up in a reasonably level position, George wandered off.

"I'm ready for some coffee. Care to join me?"

Billy Joe's face lit up. "Coffee? Sure!"

Inside the trailer, Simon gestured to the dinette. "Make yourself at home." He got down the coffee and coffee pot and was about to throw out the old grounds when Billy Joe asked, "Can I have the grounds?"

Simon looked up in surprise. The boy, for Simon judged him to be about nineteen, blushed and looked down at his hands. "We always use the grounds a couple of times, then they go in the garden."

Simon dumped the grounds in a plastic bag, suddenly glad he'd bought more coffee the day before. He made the coffee, then took a dozen eggs and a pound of bacon out of the refrigerator. He looked for bread, then remembered he'd given it to Meg. He dug into the sack of groceries for a fresh loaf.

He started half of the bacon frying and poured them each a mug of coffee. He sipped his at the stove while he cooked. He divided the bacon between two plates, cooked a couple of eggs apiece and carried the plates over to the table, sliding one in front of Billy Joe.

The boy gave him a quick, shy look and proceeded to wolf down the food. They ate in silence. When they finished, Simon carried the plates to the sink and put them to soak, then refilled their coffee mugs.

"How long have you been camping here?" Simon asked.

"You ain't gonna tell on us, are you?"

"Why should I?"

"Well, this here is private land. Owned by a fellow in town. If he knew we was here, he'd chase us off." He gave Simon a defiant look. "We like it here and we ain't hurting nobody."

Simon shrugged. It wasn't his concern and he said so. "How'd you find this place?" he asked, more out of curiosity than concern.

"I guess Andy found it first, then Wheat. Wheat knew Lovey from someplace and brought her here when they threw her out of where she was staying. I don't know where he ran into George and Frannie. It was Frannie that brought Meg and Jamie. Buford, well, he just showed up one day."

"And you?"

"Oh, I was picking up a few dollars at a street fair up the coast. You know, singing on a street corner. The cops was rousting me 'cause I didn't have an address and didn't have a permit. I'd been living in my truck. I didn't know you had to buy a permit to participate. I was just trying to pick up a little gas and eating money. Anyway, George and Frannie had a little booth next to me. George came over and got the cops to let me alone if I quit singing, then that night they brought me up here. That was a couple of months ago."

He finished his coffee and stood up. "You fixing to use those grounds again?

"What? Oh, no. You can have them."

"Thanks."

Simon watched him carefully add the grounds to those already in the plastic bag.

"What do you do all day up here?" Simon asked, his curiosity thoroughly aroused.

"Oh, we have lots to do. Right now I gotta go weed the garden."

"Want some help?"

He looked doubtfully at Simon's clean hands. "You ever weeded a garden before?"

"No, but I'm sure I can learn."

"Sure, why not. Come on."

Simon followed the boy out and was surprised to see him carry the coffee grounds across to Meg who was working beside the Buick station wagon. They talked for a moment in soft tones, then Meg looked at him and smiled. Jamie was again playing in the dirt near her mother.

He walked close enough to see that Meg was washing clothes in a bucket balanced on top of a stump. A line of what appeared to be a piece of parachute rigging had been strung between two trees and held several articles of clothing including a pair of men's jeans and a flannel shirt.

He glanced in the windows of the station wagon and saw a bed of blankets in the back, with clothes and personal belongings piled neatly in the front seat. He turned away, slightly embarrassed, as if he'd be caught peeking into someone's bedroom. Which, of course, he had. He realized with a start that the station wagon *was* their home.

He followed Billy Joe across the clearing where the boy collected a couple of short handled hoes. "These are what the farm laborers used until the union made the farmers provide regular hoes. We use them because we got them for a quarter apiece."

Billy Joe led off on a narrow path through the woods. The mist was slowly burning away but the dense underbrush still dripped. The leaves and pine needles underfoot were spongy but at least the path wasn't muddy. Simon followed, but his thoughts were back in camp.

He didn't understand why the thought of the young woman and her daughter living out of their station wagon should shock him. God knows he'd seen enough of the homeless on the streets of Los Angeles. But in the city, it had just been a part of the scene, anonymous, unconnected. Something that was just *there*. These people were different.

He stopped, startled. People. These were people, real people. In Los Angeles, the homeless were just that—the homeless. Not people without homes, trying to survive the best they could, but just *the homeless*. No different from these people; no different from himself.

Yes, they were different. They had no choice. He did. He could afford a nice trailer, gas to get him wherever he wanted to go, food whenever he was hungry. He was living. These people were just surviving.

"Hey, you coming?"

Billy Joe's call snapped him out of his thoughts and he hurried down the path that ended in another small clearing. The underbrush had been cleared away and the ground worked up into a neat garden. Rows of sticks had been driven into the ground along one side with string laced between them. Green plants were twining their way up the string and sticks. He recognized the lacy tops of carrots in several more rows. He had no idea what the green leaves poking their way through the rest of the garden were. At the other end of the garden, more stakes provided support for other growth. Somewhere out of sight he heard the rush of falling water.

Billy Joe waved a hand at the first section of stakes. "Those are peas. They're already blooming so it won't be long before we'll have fresh peas. I weeded them yesterday. We've already had some radishes and onions. We've got lettuce coming and squash. Carrots, cabbage and tomatoes and some cauliflower over there."

Simon looked around in dismay. He wouldn't know a cabbage from a weed. What if he pulled up the wrong thing?

Billy Joe must have read his expression because he chuckled. "Come on, you can weed the beans. You can't go wrong there."

So you say, he thought as he followed Billy Joe to the far rows of stakes.

Billy Joe showed him bean plants and watched as he started hoeing gently around the plants. After a few minutes, Simon got the hang of it and Billy Joe left him with a slap on the back.

TWO HOURS later, he finished weeding the beans and tried to straighten up. His back screamed in pain and he had to grit his teeth to keep from crying out. How had the migrant laborers worked all day bent over in such an unnatural position? No wonder there had been strikes. He was tired, thirsty and dirty.

His hands ached and he'd developed a couple of blisters. He looked around and saw Billy Joe working a short distance away. He walked up the edge of the garden and waited until Billy Joe finished the row he was weeding.

The boy straightened slowly, working the kinks out of his back, and grinned. "You look beat."

Simon returned the grin. "I am, and thirsty, too."

"Let's go get a drink."

Simon expected him to head back for camp, but instead he entered the woods. A hundred feet or so into the woods they came on a fast running stream that spilled over a small waterfall, tumbled a few more feet to a higher waterfall that fell into a good-sized pool before dancing blithely down the mountain. A tin cup was hooked to a tree branch with an old wire hanger.

Billy Joe handed him the cup. "Go ahead. It's good, clean water. Most as good as a cold beer."

Simon banished the thought of news stories he'd read about the dangers of drinking from streams. He was too thirsty to worry about microbes or whatever. He rinsed the cup and drank long and deep. Billy Joe was almost right. It was good, cold and refreshing, but no where near as good as a cold beer. He thought of the eight cans left in the half rack in the truck.

Billy Joe drank, hung the cup back and dragged two plastic five gallons jugs from the brush. He uncapped them and set them in the gravel under the first waterfall.

"Meg and Jamie brought these up when she came after wash water this morning. I told her I'd bring them back."

While the jugs were filling, he led Simon down along the bank to the second, higher waterfall that fell into the pool. "This here's where we bathe when it's warm enough. If you see a rag tied on that branch there, back off." He gave Simon an intent look. "That means one of the women is here. We wouldn't want them to be made uncomfortable or anything."

"Understood."

They collected the water jugs and walked back to camp.

"Is Meg married?"

"Why you asking?"

"I saw the clothes on the line but Wheat didn't mention a

husband."

"Meg ain't got no way of earning money so Wheat and Andy and I give her a dollar or two from time to time to wash our duds."

Remembering the wet and dirty clothes still littering the shower floor, he asked, "Think she'd do some for me?"

"Probably. You can ask."

Billy Joe carried the water to the fire ring and Simon headed for his trailer. After an all but sleepless night, the fresh air and physical labor had left him tired and hungry. He stopped at the truck, collected the beer and carried it into the trailer and stowed it in the refrigerator.

He wanted a shower but wasn't sure how much water was left in the tank. Maybe later he'd try the creek. Too tired to cook or even make a sandwich, he rummaged through the pantry cabinet and found a can of Franco-American spaghetti. He opened it and ate it cold out of the can. After rinsing and crushing the can, he headed for the bedroom and stretched out on the bed and was instantly asleep.

It was early evening when he woke up fuzzy-headed and staggered into the bathroom. The muscles in his shoulders, arms and back ached abominably. He couldn't believe how out of shape he'd gotten in just over a month. He'd have to get back into some kind of exercise schedule soon.

Collecting the beer and a Coca Cola for Jamie from the refrigerator, he went out to join the others around the fire now blazing cheerfully in the fire ring. Simon sent a questioning look at Meg, who nodded, before giving the Coke to Jamie. Billy Joe shook his head when Simon offered him a beer. When he'd passed around the beer, he had one left. He frowned, sure that Wheat had told him there were nine people.

Wheat motioned him to a stump. Simon sat down placing the extra can on the ground and opened his beer. Wheat nodded to the extra can and said, "Lovey will be out in a minute. She's getting herself dolled up to meet you."

A large kettle, propped on rocks at the edge of the fire, was giving off a pungent odor that made Simon's stomach rumble and his mouth salivate. He saw Meg pass her beer to Billy Joe then take a sip of Jamie's Coke before leaning over to stir the kettle.

Wheat leaned over and spoke softly in Simon's ear. "We're on our own during the day but at night we kinda all chip in something and Meg cooks. That way we know she and the kid get one good meal a day."

"I'll be happy to contribute. I...."

His next words died on his lips as the door of the tiny trailer flew open and the biggest woman he'd ever seen in his life maneuvered her way to the ground and stood, arms akimbo, staring across the fire at him.

Chapter 3

WHEAT GLANCED at Simon and chuckled. "That there is Lovey Coltrane. Yessiree, that's our Lovey."

Simon watched in fascination as the woman made her way daintily toward the fire. She topped Simon's six-foot-six by at least three inches and must have weighed over three hundred pounds, yet she seemed to float across the ground with a surprising grace. She carried herself with the elegance and poise of a woman secure in her own attractiveness.

He could only stare as she came into the light. Her long skirt appeared to be made from a chenille bedspread. He couldn't see her blouse for she had several damask tablecloths draped around her as shawls.

As she settled herself on a log, his eyes traveled to her face. She had once been a beautiful woman and that beauty still lingered under the rolls of fat. Her long, black hair had been pulled into a topknot before falling in an inky cascade around her shoulders and down her back. She smiled across the fire and Simon was jolted by the wave of pure sensuousness that radiated from her.

At his side, Wheat chuckled. "Simon, meet our Lovey, Lovey Coltrane. Lovey, this here is Simon Threadneedle."

Lovey nodded. When she spoke, her voice was like sun-warmed velvet and sent a pleasant ripple up his spine.

"Threadneedle. A distinguished name. One doesn't hear it often. Threadneedle. Yes, I like it. Perhaps I will give you a reading one of these days."

Simon felt the blood rushing up his neck and into his face. "Thank you, Ma'am," he murmured, unable to think of any other response.

Buford snickered. Simon looked at him and felt an immediate antipathy. The man exuded an aura of filth that had nothing to do with the dirty clothes he was wearing or the grime imbedded in his flesh. Simon felt his own flesh crawl as he studied the other man.

The silence that had fallen on the group when Lovey appeared was broken when Andy jumped up and began kicking dirt over the fire. Meg grabbed the kettle, lifting it out of his way. George and Billy Joe finished dousing the fire as Andy slunk back into the shadows, picked up his rifle and disappeared into the woods.

Simon turned to Wheat. "What—"

"Shush!"

Simon stared at the others in the dim moonlight. Meg was clasping Jamie tightly to her chest. The others sat as if turned to stone. Then he heard the far off sound of a motor, and he, too, waited in silence. He could feel their anxiety as sound of the motor grew louder. The tension didn't ease until the sound faded away in the distance. It was several minutes before Wheat shook himself, took a deep breath and said, "Did that stew get done? We might as well eat."

George and Billy Joe left the circle and returned a few minutes later with a couple of Coleman lanterns. There was a general relaxation as Meg dished up the stew and Frannie handed the plates around, but the pleasure of the evening had dissipated. They ate in silence.

Frannie was collecting the plates when Andy reappeared. She filled a plate and carried it to him. Simon noted that he kept the rifle beside him as he ate. When he finished, he looked up and said, "A pickup. The same one that was by here a couple of nights ago. Three men. They went on up the mountain."

"Do you think they spotted our tracks?" Wheat asked, rolling a cigarette.

"Nope. I went down early this morning. The rain had washed them out, but we'd best sit still for a couple more days. There's still some wet spots that would leave sign if we was to go out."

Wheat turned to Simon. "I know you was figuring to leave tomorrow, but—"

"No problem. I don't mind hanging around a few more

days. If I'm going to stay, I want to contribute my share." He glanced over at Meg. "Come over in the morning and you can go through my supplies and take what you need."

He glanced around the group, his gaze stopping on Buford. The man was smirking. Why? Their gaze locked for moment and Simon was sure he read triumph in the man's eyes before they shifted away. He stood up, suddenly anxious to be away from these people. Something was going on here that he didn't understand. He wasn't sure he wanted to. "Okay if I go for a run tomorrow?" he asked.

Wheat looked up at him. "Sure. This ain't no prison camp, you know."

Andy stood up, collecting his rifle. "Just don't move the barricade and try not to leave tracks where they can be seen." Even in the dim moonlight, Simon could see that his eyes had taken on the same blank look as the first night. "They're all around. Got to be careful." He faded back into the darkness.

Wheat spoke up. "I measured your camper today and got out the wood. I'll start on your cabinet tomorrow."

"Thanks. Well, I think I'll turn in."

SIMON AWOKE the next morning to a chorus of birdcalls. He listened for several minutes wondering how long it had been since he'd heard such sweet music. Probably not since his boyhood back in Iowa. Certainly not in Nam, and he couldn't recall hearing bird song in L.A. Or maybe his ears had been so attuned to other more crucial noises that his brain had blocked the sweet sound of birds.

He dressed quickly in running shorts, tee shirt and Reeboks and stepped outside. It was just breaking daylight: the ground under the trees still in shadow. He glanced around the silent camp. Billy Joe was asleep in a sleeping bag on an old wooden army cot set up under a tarp stretched between two trees and the outside mirror of his truck. There was no sign of the others. He wondered briefly where Andy slept. In the pup tent, maybe.

Simon shivered in the cool morning air. It might be May but the nights still were cold here. Cold and damp. Wisps of mist crept along the ground like ghostly fingers. He glanced up.

Clouds obscured the tops of the trees. He shivered.

He crossed behind his truck and began to jog up the path toward the road. A quarter of a mile from camp the path was blocked by a fallen tree. He jogged in place while he surveyed the area. This must be the barricade Andy had mentioned.

The path at this point was barely a car width wide, the trees on each side so close together there was hardly room to walk between them. He jogged closer and saw a nylon fishing line attached to the fallen tree. At first glance, it appeared as if some fisherman had gotten his line tangled while climbing over the log, but a closer look revealed that one end of the line ran up a nearby tree.

Simon moved toward the tree, his gaze following the nearly invisible line, then stopped, his face splitting in a wide grin. The end of the line was tied the several tin cans. A closer look showed a handful of small pebbles in each can. Anyone attempting to move the fallen log would set up a clatter that could be heard all the way to camp. No one was going to drive into camp unexpectedly. He wondered how many other traps had been set around the camp.

He pushed his way through the heavy underbrush, moving slowly through the trees as he made his way toward the road and found several more trip wires. He had no doubt that this was Andy's work. At least none of them were aimed at causing harm, more an early warning system in case of unwanted visitors. Maybe it was just Andy's paranoia.

When he reached what passed for a road, he stopped again. It had probably once been a logging road, but was so overgrown that only two tracks showed where vehicles had clawed their way through. He looked downhill and shuddered. How in the hell had he managed to get his rig up here in the dark?

Turning, he jumped across the left track and began to jog uphill, staying on the grass and weeds in the center of the track. The road turned and twisted through heavy timber and underbrush, as it grew steadily steeper. When he finally came to a spot where the mountain fell away in a steep scree of detritus, he was gasping for air and sweating heavily. Running in place, he paused for a look.

Below him lay a sweeping view of ridge after ridge of dense forest. Far to the west, rays of the rising sun glinted on the ocean. Captured by the beauty of the scene, he stopped running and seated himself on a boulder. He sat for a long time drawing the fresh, clean air into his lungs while his spirit drank in the beauty and serenity. A chipmunk paused while crossing the scree to study him. He watched two squirrels playing tag in a tree.

A jay scolding him from a nearly branch finally made him aware of his stiffening muscles. Reluctantly he heaved himself up and began to walk slowly back down the trail, filled with a contentment he hadn't know in years.

He looked about him in wonder. The giant ferns, the huge trees covered with moss, the abundance of vegetation were almost primeval and filled him with awe. There was something intriguing, almost magical about this place. The harsh world of Los Angeles with its dirt and smog, its tensions, suspicions and violence seemed unreal, a nightmare.

He wouldn't be leaving tomorrow. He'd stay as long as possible, as long as they'd let him.

The camp was coming awake when he got back. He stopped at his trailer long enough to collect a towel, soap, clean sweats and change his running shoes for a pair of thongs then headed for the creek. As he crossed the camp, Meg came out of the woods. She smiled and said, "Good morning."

Simon returned her smile. "I'm going to try out your bathing facilities. As soon as I get back, we'll go through my supplies."

"Are you sure? I mean, we'd all appreciate it but—"

"I'm sure. It's so beautiful here I'd like to stay a while, if it would be all right."

"You'd be more than welcome, I'm sure."

Billy Joe was weeding as Simon walked around the garden. They both nodded but neither spoke.

At the pool, Simon draped his towel and clean clothes over a bush, stripped, and grasping the bar of soap, stepped into the pool. "Jesus!" he gasped as the icy cold water numbed his feet.

A low chuckle erupted from behind him but before he could turn, a brown body flashed past him in a shallow dive, splashing him. Shivering uncontrollably, he started to back out of the water when Andy's head popped up.

"Go for it, man, it's the only way to do it," Andy said. The grin faded as he stared at scars that decorated Simon's body.

"Looks like you've seen some action, too. Nam?"

Simon nodded. Some of the scars were from Viet Nam and he saw no reason to explain the most recent ones. Embarrassed by the other's intent stare, Simon took a deep breath and plunged into the water and came up gasping. The water was deeper than it had looked and he found himself up to his armpits. Teeth chattering, he asked, "Does it ever warm up?"

"Nah. Invigorating, ain't it?"

"That isn't exactly the word I'd use," he replied, struggling toward the waterfall. He hurriedly soaped his body and hair, then stepped under the falling water to rinse himself. His skin was blue with cold as climbed out of the pool and grabbed his towel.

Andy was floating on his back, the grin back on his face. "Hey, you want to share your soap?"

Simon tossed him the bar. "Keep it. I've got more."

He rubbed himself roughly to stimulate his circulation then climbed into his sweats, anxious for the warmth they provided.

He was halfway back to camp before he realized Andy was right, he did feel remarkably refreshed and invigorated. He also realized that he was enjoying himself more than he had in a long time.

For years his only friends had been in the tight knit law enforcement community. He'd had little social contact with civilians. One of the penalties of a career in law enforcement was seeing too much of the worst of society. It bred an automatic distrust that made relating to ordinary people difficult.

He liked it here and he liked these people. It wouldn't be easy to overcome twenty-five years of suspicion and isolation but this was his chance to get to know ordinary people in ordinary situations. He'd seen too much of the underside of life: the greed, the hate, the lies, and the violence. Here was his chance to be accepted for himself. He just hoped to hell he wouldn't blow it.

Jamie was crouched at the edge of the clearing drawing

pictures in the dirt. Curious, he stopped and knelt beside the girl. She tensed and scratched out the picture she had drawn, but not before Simon had caught a quick look at the stick figures: a man holding a stick, a woman covering her head and a child crouched between them.

"Hi. My name is Simon. I hear you like peanut butter."

The girl ignored him, digging in the dirt with the point of her stick.

"What else do you like besides peanut butter? How about chocolate? Do you like chocolate?"

Jamie jumped up and ran across the camp to where her mother was filling a large blue-enameled coffee pot with water. Simon followed and saw that Meg was scraping the used grounds he'd given Billy Joe the day before into the pot.

"I've got almost a full two pound can of coffee. Come on over and I'll give it to you."

She looked up. "We'd be obliged. We've been out of coffee for several days."

"Billy Joe tells me you do laundry. Would you do some for me? I'll be happy to pay you."

She smiled and Simon was touched by the sweetness of the smile. "Sure. Just let me put this on the fire and start some water heating."

When she had the coffee pot settled on stones in the fire ring, he poured water from a water can into a metal bucket and carried it to the fire for her. She followed him into his trailer and gazed around appreciation.

Simon dumped his dirty clothes in a pile by the door and began opening cabinets. He turned around to see Meg running a hand over the front of the oven.

"Do you like to bake? You're welcome to use the oven anytime."

She jerked her hand away and looked up at him. "Do you mean it? I tried making biscuits in Frannie's Dutch oven on the fire, but they didn't come out too good. Frannie said I needed self-rising flour."

"I don't have any of that, but I do have a box of Bisquick here someplace." He turned back to the cabinets. "There's some cocoa, flour, macaroni. Here, you have a look. Take whatever you think you can use."

Hesitantly, Meg began to sort through his stock of groceries. He dug out a paper sack and began bagging the items she selected.

"Oh, canned milk! I can make Jamie hot chocolate tonight. But you need it for your coffee."

"No, I like my coffee black. Go ahead and take it; take the cocoa and sugar, too."

He filled several filters with coffee and put them in the refrigerator, then handed her the coffee can. "By the way, that stew last night was delicious. What was in it? It didn't taste like chicken."

"Rabbit. Andy and Billy Joe catch them in snares. We eat a lot of rabbit and squirrel. Frannie and George take the bones."

Bones? Simon shuddered and decided not to ask.

He carried the supplies to her car while she carried his clothes. As he started back to his trailer, Frannie waved him over to where she seated on a stump working at a jerry-built table. When he got close, he saw what he taken to be bits of plastic were really small animal bones. The vise attached to the plank in front of her held a tiny bone. She was delicately drilling out the marrow. A battered and scratched attaché case sat open on the ground beside her. Laid out inside on a piece of red felt were several necklaces made from polished bones.

"There's a street fair in Lion Rock this weekend. We'll have our booth."

"You sell this stuff?"

"Sure. Been doing it for years. We used to hit all the fairs and flea markets."

"Can you make a living at it?"

She shrugged. "We get by, long as we don't have to pay rent. Used to be better. Now, we sell mostly to tourists."

She glanced up at him. "I see you gave Meg some groceries. That was nice of you."

It was his turn to shrug. "I like it here. I'd like to stay awhile."

"You're welcome to come into town with us on Saturday.

Billy Joe got him a gig at that bar at the edge of town. Lovey will be coming, too."

"What does she sell?"

Frannie laughed. "She tells fortunes, reads Tarot cards and palms." She looked up at him, eyes dancing. "She's good."

"What about the rest? Will they be going to town, too?"

"No. Andy never goes to town. Neither does Meg. One of us does their shopping for them. Wheat might change his mind and go, but I doubt it. He won't have no money 'till the first."

"Buford?"

She shrugged and went back to working on the bone. "You can ride with us if you want. We try not to take more than two cars out at once. It'll be kinda crowded. Lovey will ride with us. Maybe you better go with Billy Joe."

"Let me think about it."

"Sure."

THE NEXT few days passed pleasantly enough. Simon jogged every morning, learned to like the fog and drizzle that occurred most days, grew used to the icy bath, helped weed the garden and haul water. Only once was their peace disturbed by the return of the three men in the pickup.

Wheat finished the storage locker for Simon's pickup. There was no doubt that Wheat was an artisan. Simon told him that the locker was almost too beautiful to use for the storage of tools.

"Well now, as my pa always said, *if you're going to do something, do it right or don't bother to do it at all.*" Wheat studied his creation and shook his head. "It really needs a couple of coats of marine varnish, but I ain't got any."

"I could pick some up in town tomorrow."

"You do that, son, and I'll give her several coats before we put her in your truck. You going with Billy Joe?"

"I thought we'd take my truck if Billy Joe's agreeable. I need to gas up."

Saturday morning the camp was astir well before daylight. Simon had just finished the last of his coffee when Billy Joe rapped on his door and stuck his head in. "Can I load Lovey's stuff in the back of your truck?"

"Sure," Simon replied, swallowing the last of the coffee and putting the cup in the sink. "I'll give you a hand."

The first thing he noticed when they left the trailer was the absence of the old Plymouth and stopped, staring at the empty space. Billy Joe followed his stare and said, "Buford packed up and pulled out about midnight."

Simon followed Billy Joe to Lovey's trailer, helped him pull a long, tarpaulin wrapped bundle from underneath and carry it to his truck.

"I can get the rest," Billy Joe said.

Simon wandered over to where Wheat and Andy were standing with Meg. She held out a list and the five dollars that Simon had paid her for doing his laundry.

"Could you pick up these things for me?"

Simon took the list and the money. "Of course. Are you sure you don't want to come with us?"

Meg took a quick step back. "No! Oh, no. Excuse me, I think Jamie is waking up." She turned and hurried back to the station wagon. Simon watched her walk away, then turned back to find both men looking at him.

He raised an eyebrow. "What?"

"You won't tell anyone where we're staying or who's here, will you?" Wheat asked.

"No, of course not."

Andy handed him a list and some money. "I'll go move the barricade."

As Andy moved off through the shadows, Simon asked, "Wheat, what's Meg scared of?"

"Who says she's scared?"

"I do."

"Well, I reckon that's her business."

Simon continued to stare at the old man, who finally shrugged and said, "I don't know for sure. She ain't said, but I'm guessing she's running from a mean husband or boyfriend. When Frannie brought them up here, they'd both been beaten up pretty bad. Maybe you ain't noticed, but that little girl don't talk. She ain't said word one since she's been here."

Before Simon could answer, Billy Joe came up. "You ready? We'll follow George, since you don't know the road. We want to get out on the highway before it gets light."

THE DRIVE down the narrow track was a nightmare. How in the world had he ever gotten his rig up it? Even more frightening, how was he going to get it down? At last, they turned onto the gravel road and, finally, the highway.

The sky had lightened from cobalt to cerulean blue and the few high clouds were striped with pink and gold by the time George pulled into a restaurant parking lot at the edge of town. Simon parked alongside.

Frannie was helping Lovey out of their truck. Simon got his first good look at her in her finery. His eyes widened and he bit back a grin. A damask tablecloth, dyed purple, was draped Indian sari style around her generous figure. A white blouse was barely visible under a tie-dyed length of muslin that served as a shawl. Her long hair spread over her shoulders like a black cape and was topped with a purple turban. A tarnished necklace with a huge paste ruby dangled across her forehead. Her brown eyes were heavily lined with kohl, the lashes stiff with mascara.

She entered the café ahead of them, with majestic unconcern at the startled look of the waitress and the stares of the few customers. She selected a table and waited while George set two chairs side by side at the head of the table and held them for her. Once seated on the two chairs, she smiled at them and took the menu the waitress handed her.

George and Simon exchanged a look as they sat down and Simon had a hard time controlling the laughter that bubbled in his throat.

By the time they'd eaten and gotten back in their trucks, it was full daylight. Merchants were setting up tables and racks on the sidewalk. Once they reached the park, other vehicles were being unloaded and booths of all kinds being erected on the grass in spaces marked and numbered with chalk.

George went off and returned with two pieces of cardboard. "We're in space twelve and, Lovey, you're in space fourteen."

"But I asked for thirteen."

"No thirteen. They skipped it. Numbers skip from twelve to fourteen. Guess they're superstitious."

Lovey frowned. "This is not a good omen."

Billy Joe nudged Simon. "Let's get Lovey set up."

The long, tarp wrapped bundle turned out to be a small tent painted bright crimson with the words, *MADAM ZURA, SEER OF THE EAST* painted in gilt-edged black letters. They pitched the tent, then carried in a round folding table, a footlocker, a huge wooden folding chair obviously custom-built to take Lovey's massive bulk, and an ordinary folding chair.

They left Lovey draping the table with a fringed cloth and went to help Frannie and George. Their green and white striped canvas awning looked almost sedate next to the Lovey's crimson flamboyance. They carried two long folding tables and a couple of green and white folding lawn chairs and set them up. By the time Frannie had their bone jewelry attractively displayed tourists were already strolling through the area.

Simon glanced at Billy Joe. "I could use another cup of coffee. How about you?"

"Sure. I ain't got nothing to do until tonight."

They spent the morning exploring the town. Simon's first impression, on the trip to pick up the water pump with Wheatly, had been of an attractive, stable little community. Now, walking down the main street, he saw signs of decline and decay. Empty stores predominated. He turned up the hill and strolled through the residential district. Here, too, were signs that the town was in the throes of recession. Empty houses with weathered For Sale signs were numerous. Broken foundations on a mud-scarred block were mute testimonies to an old mudslide.

They split up when Simon walked down the hill to the riverfront. He strolled to the end of one of the piers and watched sea gulls wheeling in the air, then ambled back to where two old men were fishing.

"Catching anything?"

"Not much," one answered.

He nodded toward the empty buildings that lined the waterfront. "Looks like business hasn't been too good lately."

"Nope," one of them answered. "First the fishing went to

hell, now the logging."

"Looks like somebody's doing okay," Simon said, gesturing toward the one building that was still well maintained and surrounded by what appeared to be a new chain-link fence. It had its own private dock with an enclosed boathouse on one side and a covered walkway leading to building.

"I reckon Avery Tredmore's doing okay. He's still running a couple of boats."

The other old man nudged the speaker then shot a glance at Simon. "How come you're so interested?"

Simon shrugged. "Just making conversation."

"Well make it someplace else. You're scaring the fish away."

As Simon left, he heard the grumpy fellow say, "You'd best not let Avery hear you talking about his business."

The comment piqued Simon's interest. He casually studied the building as he passed by. There was no sign of life, but on the uphill side a semi was backed halfway into a open bay. There was no advertising on the trailer and he was too far away to read the lettering on the tractor door. He continued up the hill.

At the hardware store, Simon picked up the marine varnish and a couple of items from Andy's list. At a variety store he bought a box of Crayolas and a coloring book for Jamie, then wandered back toward the park. He dropped his purchases at the truck and strolled across the grass. The park was crowded with tourists. Everyone seemed to be enjoying the day. He passed booths of all kinds, stopped to watch a glassblower making small animals, strolled through several exhibits of paintings. A table of rag dolls caught his attention. He thought of Jamie playing in the dirt and realized the little girl probably didn't have a single toy. He crossed to the booth and was greeted by a gray-haired lady with a ruddy face and twinkling eyes. She could have stepped out of a Rockwell painting.

He bought a Raggedy Ann doll and was about to turn away when he noticed a flier lying on the edge of the table. He glanced at it, and then took a longer look and his gut tightened. Below the large words HAVE YOU SEEN was a picture of Meg and Jamie.

Chapter 4

TUCKING THE doll under his arm, Simon headed for Frannie's booth. Several customers were fingering the jewelry as both Frannie and George kept an eagle eye on them. Simon waited impatiently in the back of the booth until the customers thinned. George turned to grin at him. "I see Grandma Beatty got her claws into you."

"I bought it for Jamie. I thought she might like it. You don't see many of these homemade dolls anymore."

George laughed. "That ain't home-made. She buys them by the gross. They're made in China."

"Never mind the doll." Simon lowered his voice. "Have you seen the flier?"

George frowned. "Yeah. Fellow was by here a few minutes ago with one. Where'd you see it?"

"When I bought the doll."

"You didn't say anything, did you?"

"Of course not. I didn't read it, just saw the picture. What does it say?"

George picked a crumpled ball of paper from the ground and handed it to Simon as Frannie hissed at him. "Here, you read it. I got to help Frannie." He moved up to the table where several tourists were examining the jewelry.

Simon sat down in one of the chairs and smoothed the paper over his knee. The flier gave very little information, stating only that Margaret and Jamie Poindexter had disappeared from their home in Portland on the 12th of March and that a five hundred dollar reward was being offered for information on their whereabouts. Anyone having information should contact Wesley Poindexter at the listed address and telephone number in Portland. Simon folded the flier and put it in his back pocket.

He wanted to talk to Frannie, to learn more about how she

had met Meg, but now was definitely not the time. Leaving the doll on the chair, he stood up and said, "It's after noon. What do you do about lunch? You must be getting hungry."

"One of us usually gets take-out but we've been too busy," Frannie said. "Not that I'm complaining. Business has been good."

"Tell me what you want and I'll go get it."

"Thanks. There's a hot dog stand over by the street and a beer booth." She handed him a ten from the cash box. "A couple of dogs and a beer apiece will be fine."

The line in front of Lovey's tent had disappeared so he stuck his head in and got her order. On his walk to and from the food booths he saw several more of the fliers being trampled under the feet of the browsers, but a couple of booths had posted them and several had been tacked to trees.

He delivered the food to George and Frannie. A note reading "Out To Lunch" was pinned to the door of Lovey's tent. He nudged the flap aside and went in. Lovey had removed the cloth from the table and covered it with newspapers. He put the food on the table and asked, "Mind if I join you?"

"Please do."

He reached in his pocket for the flier but before he could pull it out she held up a hand. "No. First we eat."

They polished off the hot dogs and beer in silence. When they had finished, Lovey hoisted herself out of the chair, rolled the trash in the newspapers, and said, "Wait here." Carrying the trash, she left the tent.

It was close to half an hour before she returned. Easing down into the chair, she said with a heavy sigh, "Those portable toilets are designed for midgets." As Simon started to speak, she again held up a hand. "Wait."

She replaced the fringed cloth, set a crystal ball and pack Tarot cards to one side, then settled back and said, "You've come about the fliers."

"How did you know?"

"Madam Zura knows all." She raked him with an amused glance. "You don't believe that?" She chuckled, a deep, infectious sound that had Simon grinning before he realized it.

"Actually, someone already gave me one."

"It's—"

She motioned him to silence, all the humor drained from her face. "Give me your hand," she snapped, leaning forward and rolling her eyes toward the wall of the tent. Simon saw the shadow and placed his hand on the table.

When she picked it up, Simon felt a tingle run down his spine. She ran a finger over his palm. "Ah, yes. I see you have had much trouble in your life. You have lost a loved one." She leaned forward and whispered, "Say nothing. We will talk tonight." She continued in a singsong voice, "You have lived through much danger, but more awaits you. Still, you will have a long life." Her fingers tightened on his hand and she looked up at him, frowning. "Things are not always what they seem."

She continued to stare at him for a moment, then looked back at his hand. Her frown deepened. "There will be pain and suffering for those around you. Evil is lurking but good will prevail. You are hiding something." She glanced at him from under lowered eyelids with a hint of mischief. "Soon you will meet a woman, a woman who will bring much joy into your life." She dropped his hand. "That will be five dollars."

Simon reached for his wallet, and despite her waving his money away, dropped a five-dollar bill on the table. The "Out to Lunch" sign had disappeared and several customers were lined up in front of the flap. He hurried around the side of the tent but whoever had been listening had disappeared into the crowd.

He strolled through the park trying to catch a glimpse of the person passing out the fliers but finally gave up. He bought another beer and walked over to the picnic area where several tables were scattered under the trees. Only one was empty and he sat down to nurse his beer. He was debating on whether to go get another one when two old men sat down across from each other at the other end of the table. Ignoring him, they began to play cribbage.

The beer and the warm air had made him sleepy. He crushed the paper cup and threw it in a trash receptacle on his way back to booths. He saw Buford talking to someone, but the crowd shifted, blocking his view of the man before Simon got a good look at him. Buford looked up and for a moment their glances met. With a startled look, Buford turned and darted away. Simon pushed his way through the crowd, but Buford had disappeared.

Where had Buford gone? Who had he been talking to? Simon didn't trust the man an inch. If Buford had seen the posters...shit.

He hurried through the crowd and waited impatiently until Frannie was free of customers to ask, "Have you see Buford here today?"

"No, why?"

"I thought I saw him a few minutes ago. How well do you know him?"

She shrugged. "About as well as I know you. Why?"

Simon debated telling her his opinion of Buford. If he was wrong, it would only cause hard feelings. If he was right and Buford did try for the reward money, there was nothing they could do.

"No reason. I just wondered."

Collecting the doll, he went back to the truck and stretched out on the seat. He drifted off to sleep thinking of Lovey.

A LOUD BANG on the side of the truck woke him up. He sat up, rubbing the sleep out of his eyes. Billy Joe's grinning face was framed in the window. Simon unlocked the door and opened it.

"Time to get packed up," Billy Joe said.

Simon climbed out and looked around, surprised to see that it was already dusk. He couldn't believe he'd slept so long or so hard.

Frannie and George were busily packing up their gear. Lovey's chairs, table and footlocker were sitting outside the tent, but there was no sign of Lovey. Billy Joe and Simon took down the tent, rolled it in its protective tarp and stowed it in the back of the truck. Lovey strolled by carrying her turban. Whether it was the result of the long day or just the dim light, she looked old and tired. Her movements were slow and awkward as she climbed into George's truck. By the time they had all of Lovey's gear packed, George came over carrying Billy Joe's guitar case.

"We're heading back," George said. "See you later."

Simon watched them drive away, then turned to Billy Joe. "Got time for dinner before you go to work? My treat."

"Hey, sure."

"Good. My taste buds are craving a nice thick, juicy steak. Know where we can get one?"

"Bastian's. It's out of town about a mile. Can't guarantee how good their steaks are, but they're big."

Over dinner, Simon said, "You're a long way from Kentucky. How'd you get way out here?"

"Didn't care much for the man my ma married after Pa was kilt. He got me on at the mine, but I hated it. It was the mine that kilt Pa. Anyway, soon as I'd saved up enough for that truck, I taken off. Didn't figure Nashville was ready for me." The boy grinned. "So I just headed west for California, but sorta got sidetracked. I'll get down there one of these days."

It was nearly nine o'clock and full dark when Simon pulled up in front of Slattery's LOG JAM half a mile out of town. The gravel parking lot was already full with pickup trucks and four-wheel drive vehicles predominating.

As Billy Joe climbed out, Simon said, "I'm going to stock up on groceries before the store closes. I'll see you later."

He drove back to town, found the one super market, collected a grocery cart and began cruising the aisles. He loaded the cart with staples: flour, corn meal, biscuit mix, rice, several kinds of dried beans, salt, seasonings, condiments, sugar, ten two-pound cans of coffee, cocoa for Jamie, boxes of hot and cold cereal, jars of peanut butter and jelly, canned milk and a couple of dozen cans of vegetables. On the top of the cart he balanced two styrofoam coolers. Parking the cart near the checkout counter, he got a second cart and headed for the meat counter where he selected several large roasts, slabs of ribs and a couple of chickens. From the dairy case, he added two gallons of milk, butter and orange juice. In the produce section he collected potatoes, carrots, cabbage, turnips, onions, lettuce, tomatoes, sacks of apples and of oranges. Finally, slightly embarrassed, he found the feminine items Meg had listed.

He hadn't shopped like this since Anna Marie and Orin had been kids. They weren't kids anymore. Both were married with lives of their own. Anna Marie had kids. For a moment he felt old but he shrugged the feeling away.

He found he was thoroughly enjoying himself.

The last items to go on the cart were two sacks of ice and two half racks of beer. Maneuvering the two carts was an awkward business, but he finally got them lined up at the counter. He flinched when the clerk read off the total. He'd have to find an ATM machine before long.

With the help of a bag boy, he got the carts out to his truck. The store was closing by the time he'd sorted through the sacks and stored the perishables in the coolers with the ice. His was the last vehicle in the parking lot when he finally had the rest of the groceries loaded in the camper.

As he pulled into the street, a pair of headlights came on farther down the block and followed him onto the highway. A quiver of suspicion shot through him as the headlights followed him down the highway. He shrugged it off. This wasn't L.A. and he wasn't a cop anymore. Still he felt a twinge of relief as he turned into the LOG JAM's parking lot and the car continued down the road. His brief glimpse told him only that it was a big four-door car, dark in color.

The parking lot was almost full. He found a spot at the far end of the lot next to a row of stunted and misshaped trees. After locking the truck, he weaved his way through the maze of vehicles and entered the roadhouse.

Clouds of smoke greeted him. The rumble of conversation that nearly drowned out the jukebox where Willie and Waylon beseeched mamas not to let their babies grow up to be cowboys. A dozen or so couples danced on the tiny dance floor.

Simon pushed his way through the crowd to the bar and ordered a beer. The bartender slapped a bottle of Bud in front of him. He would have preferred a Heineken or a Beck's but doubted this bar stocked anything but domestic brands. Holding the bottle, he turned his back to the bar and surveyed the room, glad he was wearing jeans and a flannel shirt. He appeared to be the only bare-headed man in the place. Everyone else seemed to be wearing either cowboy hats or baseball caps. Most of the caps displayed advertising of some kind and were worn with the bill forward.

He recognized the three loggers that had been in the diner where he and Wheat had stopped for burgers. They were sitting at a table near the dance floor deep in conversation. He looked around but didn't see Billy Joe.

Someone pulled the plug on the jukebox. The dancers straggled off the floor. A spotlight highlighted a minuscule stage containing a microphone and a barstool. The noise level sank from ear-splitting to a gentle murmur. A minute later, Billy Joe came out of back hall carrying his guitar and crossed to the stage. After adjusting the microphone, he perched on the stool, strummed a few chords and began singing.

The kid was good. Damn good. Not that Simon was any connoisseur of country music. He preferred Dixieland jazz, but the kid certainly had something. Something more than just a great voice: there was a magnetism about him when he sang. Simon lost himself in the music and wasn't aware of finishing his beer until the bartender tapped him on the shoulder. He handed the man the empty and nodded for another one.

The set finished and the spotlight went out. There was a moment of silence, and then the room reverberated with thunderous applause. Billy Joe hopped down off the stage, but before he'd taken more than couple of steps, a woman dashed up and threw her arms around his neck. More women crowded onto the dance floor. Billy Joe was grinning, but even from a distance, Simon could see the grin was forced and there was a panicked look in the kid's eyes.

The scene reminded him of pictures he'd seen of the crowds that had surrounded the Beatles and Elvis years before. But these weren't teenagers, these were mature women. A low masculine growl began to build.

The muscles in the back of Simon's neck tightened. Trouble was brewing and could explode at any moment. He'd seen it happen too many times. It had to be stopped before it erupted into violence.

Still carrying his beer, Simon weaved his way through the

tables. Before he could reach the dance floor, two of the women had gotten into a hair-pulling fight. Ahead of him a tough looking bruiser stood up and yelled, "Betty, get your ass back here."

Simon followed in the wake of the big man as he pushed his way through the women. The man grabbed a blonde who was clinging to Billy Joe's arm, and cocked a fist at Billy Joe. Before he could swing, Simon darted around him, placing his big body between the man and the kid.

"Take it easy, mister."

"Who the hell are you?"

"Nobody. Better get your wife away from this brawl."

"Don't tell me what to do," the man growled.

Simon shrugged. "I'm not. Just seems a shame to see that pretty face all bruised up."

Before the man could respond, another woman grabbed Betty's hair and Simon backed away. Using his size, he forced a path to the hall, with Billy Joe tagging close behind him.

Safe in the deserted hall, Billy Joe led the way to a storeroom at the back and sank down on a metal folding chair. He pulled a red bandanna from his back pocket and wiped the sweat from his forehead before he looked up at Simon.

"Thanks," he said, with a weak grin.

Simon leaned against a stack of cartons and returned the grin. "Looks like you're a hit with the ladies."

"Sheesh. Those chicks are crazy."

"This happen often?"

"Yeah."

"Come on, I'll buy you a beer."

"No way, man. I'm not going out again until it's time to do my last set. You go ahead."

"You okay back here?"

"Yeah." He grinned up at Simon and this time the grin was real. "I keep the door locked."

Simon realized he was still clutching the bottle of Bud and handed it to Billy Joe who took it with a heartfelt thanks. "By the way, you're damned good," Simon said over his shoulder as he stepped into the hall. He waited until he heard Billy Joe snap the lock. He was grinning as he walked down the hall and into the barroom. The kid really was good. He was no expert on that kind of music but he knew talent when he heard it. With any kind of break, Billy Joe could go places and he just might be able to arrange that break. At least it wouldn't hurt to give Marty Feinberg a call.

The room had cleared out a little and Simon was able to find a stool at the bar. He ordered another beer and nursed it. With Billy Joe gone and the jukebox blaring, things had settled down to normal.

He noticed the blonde was on the dance floor, snuggled up to the big guy, their feet barely moving. One of the three loggers he'd noticed earlier was harassing the waitress, but the woman seemed to be enjoying it.

By the time Billy Joe came out do his last set, the crowd had thinned even more. Simon finished his third beer and inched his way to the back hall. Billy Joe finished his last song, jumped off the stage and ran for the hall, half a dozen women in full pursuit. Simon blocked the passage until Billy Joe ducked into the store room, then ambled into the door marked *LOGS* to get rid of the beer he'd drank. The other door was labeled *CHIPS*.

Billy Joe had changed out of his flashy shirt, had his guitar packed and was waiting. He looked tired but happy. "I got paid. Let's get out of here."

They slipped out the back door and Simon led the way across the half-empty lot to his truck. He stopped so suddenly that Billy Joe bumped into him.

"Oh, shit." The passenger door had been pried open and was standing ajar. Ignoring it, he dashed to the driver's side. The door was still locked. Pulling out his keys he got the door open and felt under the seat. The gun hadn't been disturbed. He breathed a relieved sigh even as he grimaced at the open glove box and the papers and maps scattered over the floorboard.

Slamming the door, he walked to the back of the truck, stepping over the groceries that littered the gravel. The lock on the camper shell had been pried open and the contents ransacked.

He had a pretty damned good idea who done it. Buford! It was the kind of vicious trick a slime bag like Buford would pull.

"Simon!"

He turned and saw Billy Joe standing by the passenger door. He was holding the eviscerated doll.

Chapter 5

THE BAR HAD closed and the parking lot empty by the time a Sheriff's car drove in. The deputy who climbed out was nearly as tall as Simon, but lanky with rugged good looks, reminiscent of a young Gary Cooper. His hand rested on the butt of his gun as he crossed to where Simon was standing. In his other hand he carried a heavy-duty flashlight.

"You the one that called in?"

"Yes. Someone broke into my truck and trashed it." There was no point in mentioning Buford. He had no proof and to mention the man would lead to explanations that would involve the others.

The deputy pulled out a notebook and flipped it open. "Anything taken?"

"No, I don't think so. I didn't want to touch anything before you got here."

"About all I can do is take the report and give you a copy for your insurance company. I'll need to see your driver's license and registration."

Simon got his registration from the glove compartment and handed it to the officer. When he opened his wallet to get his driver's license, he kept his hand over the L.A. identification card. He didn't want Billy Joe and the others to know he was a cop, even a retired one. He was enjoying the easy camaraderie of the group and had no desire to see it replaced by wariness and tension.

After the deputy had verified his identification, Simon said, "How about taking some pictures? Just for the record."

The deputy stiffened. "You telling me how to do my job?"

Simon peered at the nameplate on the man's chest. "Why, no, Deputy Owens. Pictures would go a long way in convincing my insurance company, don't you think? Save you writing up a detailed description of the damage, too. But, whatever."

Owens hesitated a moment, eying Simon, then shrugged. "I'll get my camera."

Billy Joe said, "I'll see if I can find some wire or something to fasten the doors shut."

He wandered off toward the back of the club as the deputy returned with the Polaroid camera. At Simon's request, he took two sets of pictures, giving one set to Simon. After he left, Simon and Billy Joe picked up the spilled groceries and packed them back in the truck. The only things missing were the two half racks of beer and a sack of munchies.

Billy Joe held up the doll, pushing the stuffing inside the slit. "Did you get this for Jamie? I think Frannie can probably sew this back together."

They drove back to the camp in silence, each lost in his own thoughts. Simon was relieved that the bastard hadn't found his gun in its hidden pocket under the seat, but angry at the damage to his new truck. He didn't bother to wonder why Buford had done it. He'd seen too much wanton destruction to ever begin to understand the perverse reasoning behind such actions. At least Lovey's things hadn't been damaged.

The camp was asleep when they finally pulled in. Billy Joe helped Simon carry the perishable items into his trailer and stuff them in the refrigerator and freezer.

SIMON SLEPT late. It was nearly noon by the time he'd had his breakfast and went outside. A glance in the back of his truck showed that Billy Joe had unloaded Lovey's gear. As he walked toward the fire ring he was immediately aware of the strained atmosphere. Wheat and George were at the edge of the clearing splitting wood. They stopped when they saw Simon. Meg was seated at the fire ring beside Lovey; Jamie crouched in the dirt at her feet. She didn't look up as Simon approached, but Lovey watched him with a look in her eyes that he couldn't identify.

"Trouble is coming. Bad trouble. I've seen it. Did you bring it?" she said.

Simon smiled. "No. What I brought was a bunch of groceries." He turned to look at Meg. "Where do you want them?"

Meg looked up, her eyes wide and staring. "What?"

"I brought some groceries. Where do you want them?"

Wheat and George walked up. Wheat said, "I saw your truck. Looks like you had a some trouble, too. What happened?"

Simon shrugged. There was no point in telling them of is suspicions. It would only upset them. "Vandals. Probably kids with nothing better to do. Want to help me unload?"

The three men walked to the back of Simon's truck. Simon unwired the door and dropped the tailgate. George sucked in a breath when he saw the load. "Hey, you didn't have to do that. Why there's enough groceries here to last us a month."

Wheat said, "Looks like I'll have to make some more slings." He saw Simon's questioning look and said, "We hang our food in the trees, otherwise the bears would get it."

"Bears?"

"Sure. This ain't the city. We share these woods with all kinds of wild critters."

Simon decided the old man was pulling his leg and let the matter drop. They unloaded the truck and carried the groceries to the fire ring. Frannie came out of their tent and the three women set to work sorting the supplies. Simon was glad to see that the dazed look in Meg's eyes had been replaced with excitement.

Simon found the Crayolas and coloring book and carried them to where Jamie was crouched at the edge of the woods drawing in the dirt. She cringed as he squatted beside her.

"I see you like to draw. Why don't you try these?"

She ignored him, scratching out the stick figures she'd drawn in the dirt. He took a deep breath, held out his gift and said, "I won't hurt you, honey. I'd like to be your friend."

She continued to ignore him. With an inward sigh, he placed the book and box of colors on the ground beside her. When she made no move to either look at them or pick them up, he stood and walked back to the fire ring.

"I've got a couple of chickens in the refrigerator. How about fried chicken and gravy and biscuits tonight? You can use my oven," he said to Meg.

He turned to Frannie. "Can I see you a minute?" Simon was

surprised at the cool look she gave him, but she followed him back to his trailer. Inside, she stood with her hands on her hips, glaring at him.

"What's the matter? What have I done?" he asked.

"I suppose you think we should be grateful. We may be poor, mister, but we don't need charity. We don't need no Lord Bountiful coming in here putting us down."

Simon sank down on the banquette. "Oh, Lord. Is that how it looked?"

"Damned right."

He rubbed a hand over his face. "I'm sorry. I just wanted to contribute my share. It's...it's the first time in years I've done more than pick up some frozen dinners or hit the deli section. I guess I got carried away. I never thought how it might look."

"No, you didn't think." Her voice softened. "You ain't married?"

"My wife died ten years ago."

She sat down across from him. "No kids?"

"Two. Both married and gone."

"Tell me about them."

He hesitated a moment. "Not much to tell. Orin, my oldest, is a real estate broker in Seattle. Has his own agency. Married. No kids. Anna Marie is a teacher; her husband is a computer programmer. They live in Denver and have two children, girls."

"So you don't see much of them."

"No, they have their own lives."

"Must be lonely. That why you live in a trailer?"

"No. Yes. Not really. I retired last month and decided to do something I've always wanted to do, see this country. No itinerary, no time table."

They sat in silence for a few minutes, then Frannie asked, "What did you want to see me about?"

"Oh, yeah." He got up and retrieved the doll from where he'd stuffed in a drawer the night before and handed it to her. "Billy Joe thought you might be able to mend this."

She studied the slit for a moment. "The vandals did this? Sick! Yeah, I think I can fix it."

She started to get up but Simon put out a hand to stay her.

"Wait. I understand you brought Meg here. How did you meet her?"

"Why do you want to know?"

"I like her. I'd like to be her friend. She's in some kind of trouble. You saw the flier. I'd like to help if I can."

"I don't know what you can do."

"I won't know either unless I know what the trouble is."

"Well, I can't help you 'cause I don't know. She was scared, tired and hungry when I met her. She'd stopped at a cove up the road a way. George and I stopped to hunt shells and we got to talking, or at least I did. She didn't have much to say, but she and Jamie were both covered with bruises. She said she was planning to camp there for a few days. Thing is, the cops check that cove frequently. Kids like to go there for beer busts."

Frannie shifted on the seat. "Not that she said anything, but I've seen battered women before. So I brought them up here. That's all I know, except they're both scared out of their wits. Neither of them has left the camp in two months. That little girl ain't spoke a word in all that time, but she has nightmares. Screaming meemie nightmares."

She left with the doll and Simon sat for several minutes thinking about what she'd said.

WHEAT BANGED on the side of the trailer, then opened the door and stuck his head in. "You get the varnish?"

"What? Oh, yes, it's in the truck."

After he'd given the varnish to Wheat, he looked around the camp. Meg and Lovey were tying the groceries into bundles and hoisting them into a tree. He smiled when he saw Jamie seated in the dirt, head bent over the coloring book, intently coloring away. Billy Joe was up and drinking coffee at the fire. Simon strolled over and poured himself a cup.

"Where's George and Andy?"

"George is gathering wood. I don't know where Andy is. Off in the woods playing soldier, I guess."

Simon finished the coffee and tossed the dregs in the fire. "I'll go help George."

"Hang on a minute and I'll go with you."

Later that night, comfortably full of fried chicken, biscuits and country gravy, they sat around the fire. Billy Joe got out his guitar and they sang songs, old camp songs and some from the sixties. They'd just finished a chorus of *Blowing in the Wind*, when Andy shushed them. He disappeared into the woods.

Billy Joe jumped up and began to kick dirt into the fire. Everyone sat in silence, ears strained. Soon Simon heard the sound of the motor. Eventually it faded into the distance and Andy returned to tell them it was the same truck.

"Where do you suppose they go?" Frannie asked. "That ain't nothing but an old logging road. It don't go nowhere."

Simon glanced at Andy. He had an idea that Andy knew exactly where the men went and what they were doing. He didn't think there was much that happened on this mountain that Andy didn't know about.

Andy quirked an eyebrow at Simon's questioning look and shrugged. "I seen their truck on the way out a couple of times, loaded with tree bark and ferns."

Later Simon took Andy aside. "You know what's going on up there?"

Andy looked at him with a steely gaze. Simon held eye contact. Andy shrugged and said, "Best you don't know."

"I think I can guess. Those loggers have found a new money crop. Do the others know?"

"Wheat does. You gonna turn them in?"

Simon shook his head. "Not my business."

Andy stared at him for a moment then turned and walked into the woods.

IT WAS BARELY daylight when Simon awoke and slipped into his running gear. The camp was still asleep when he left his trailer. He stretched, breathing deeply of the cool air, and was about to jog out of the camp when his glance lit on a white bundle at the foot of a tree. He trotted across for a better look.

His first thought was that Wheat hadn't been kidding about bears. He gazed anxiously around. The only bear he'd ever seen was in a zoo, behind a moat and a sturdy fence. He remembered the teeth and claws and shuddered. He had no desire to meet one face to face.

He picked up the rope, planning to hoist the bundle back into the tree, then stopped, and examined the rope. It hadn't been gnawed or torn; it had been untied. Bears couldn't untie knots.

He knelt beside the bundle and began to go through it. Someone had opened the sacks of apples and oranges, removed a few and refastened the sacks. Whoever had taken the fruit had done it during the night. Why? The food was there for them all. There was no need to steal. And why hadn't the pilferer hung the sack back in the tree?

Unless...He sank back on his heels and studied the camp. Had his movements inside the trailer scared the person away?

He stood and walked over to Wheat's truck and tapped on the camper door. After a minute he tapped louder and felt movement within. The door opened and Wheat stuck his head out.

"Shit, it ain't even daylight yet."

"Sure it is, Wheat. Best part of the day. Come on out. There's something you need to see."

"Trouble?"

Simon shrugged. "You'll have to tell me."

"Lemme get my boots on."

Before they were halfway across the clearing, Wheat spied the bundle. "Oh, shit. He's struck again. What'd he take this time?"

"Apples and oranges from this sack. I don't know about the others. Meg will probably know. Do you know who did it?"

"Not exactly."

"But it's happened before?"

"Yeah. He never takes much."

"Who?"

Wheat shrugged. "Andy says there's an old man living somewhere up the mountain. Got him a hidey-hole, but Andy ain't found it yet. Andy says he's harmless and to leave him be."

"But he steals from your camp."

"Yeah, but like I say, he don't take much." He shrugged again and asked, "You got any coffee going? Wake a man in the middle of the night, least you could do was offer him a cuppa coffee."

"Come on, you old coot, I'll make a pot."

THE CAMP was stirring as Simon started for his run. Several days before, he'd found a deer trail that led along the side of the mountain. It had become his favorite place to run, being fairly level and protected from the frequent drizzle by the thick canopy of tree branches. As he jogged back to camp, moving silently on the springy carpet of pine needles, he decided it was time he moved on. He needed to report the damage to his truck and get it repaired.

The sound of a motor stopped him in his tracks. He paused beside a tree, waiting for the sound to fade away. It didn't. In the sudden silence, Simon realized the truck had stopped. A few minutes later he heard the rattle of Andy's early warning system and a man cursing.

He came to the road and saw a pickup truck parked near the turnoff to the camp. He crouched behind a bush until he was sure there was no one in the truck, then crossed the road in three giant steps, and began to work his way silently through the woods.

He heard angry voices before he could see the camp. He stopped in the shadows at the edge of the clearing.

Three loggers stood near the fire ring facing Billy Joe, Frannie and George. Lovey was standing next to her trailer, Meg beside her clutching a terrified Jamie. He didn't see either Wheat or Andy.

The men were the same three men he'd seen the first day, and again in the tavern. The one in center was saying, "...out of here today."

Frannie stepped forward. "We ain't hurting nobody."

"This is private land."

"It ain't your land. Who are you to tell us we got to go?"

"Pete, show the bitch we mean business."

Pete stepped forward and swung a booted foot at the kettle simmering on the fire, kicking it over and spilling the pot of beans into the fire. Another kick sent the coffee pot bouncing across the ground.

Billy Joe let out a growl and charged Pete. The scrap lasted only a few seconds. The kid was game but no match for the big logger. Two swift blows and Billy Joe collapsed in the dirt. George, fists clenched, took a step forward but Frannie grabbed his arm and clung to him.

Pete grinned. "That's right, lady. Hang on to him or I'll give him some of the same." He turned to the man in the middle. "Hey, Frenchie, let's teach these folks a lesson. What'da you say."

He pulled knife from his belt, crossed to the tree and slashed the ropes that held the food supplies. As the bundles dropped, the third man joined him and they kicked and stomped the bundles.

Meg began to cry. Frenchie took a step toward her and said, "Shut up, bitch, or I'll give you something to cry about. Hey, you're kinda cute. Come on out here so's I can get a look at you."

An anger he hadn't felt in years raged through Simon and he charged out of the shadows, taking Frenchie down in a tackle that would have done a Seahawk linebacker proud. He rolled away and came to his feet in one smooth move. He stood, fists clenched, while the logger got to his feet. They were nearly the same size although Frenchie was a good thirty years younger.

He grinned at Simon. "Well, now, grandpa. Think you can take me?"

He threw a punch that Simon easily avoided. Then, before Frenchie could recover, Simon whirled and sent the logger head over heels with a karate kick. The third logger charged. Pete yelled, "Take him, Stan." Simon met Stan halfway, took a blow on the shoulder, then threw him with a flying mare.

All of the skills he'd acquired in his years with Delta Force came back. He fought with a blind fury. For the next few minutes, he gave the loggers a good drumming, but his age soon began to tell. He wasn't as quick or as agile as he'd been at twenty-five. He realized with exasperation that he was in for a beating.

He backed away trying to control his breathing as the three started toward him. Suddenly they stopped, staring past him. He risked a glance over his shoulder. Andy stood behind him, the AK-47 cradled in his arms. Slowly he raised it, the barrel looking as big as a cannon as it aimed at them.

Andy's eyes held the same blank look Simon had seen the first night. Simon hastily moved out of the line of fire.

The three men began to back away, their hands outspread. The muzzle of the gun followed them. At the edge of the clearing, they broke and ran. Frenchie called back, "You ain't seen the last of us. We'll get you."

Simon saw Andy's finger tighten on the trigger and hissed, "No. Let them go."

Andy didn't take his finger off the trigger until they heard the motor of the truck rev and the squeal of tires. Gradually the blank look faded from his eyes and he blinked, visibly relaxing.

For several minutes no one moved. Billy Joe shifted on the ground, breaking the paralysis that gripped them. Frannie knelt beside the groaning boy. Meg loosened her hold on Jamie and the child ran to the car, crawled inside and burrowed into the sleeping bag, pulling it over her head.

Lovey sighed. "We'd better see how much damage those bastards did. Come on, Meg."

The two women crossed to the bundles and began to sort through the groceries, trying to salvage as much as they could.

Simon glanced around as George came up. For the first time, he noticed Wheat's truck was gone. "Where's Wheat?"

George shrugged. "I don't know. He took off real early. Didn't say where he was going."

"What's the date?" Andy asked, propping the gun against a tree and crossing to help Meg hoist a bundle into the tree.

"June third," Simon answered.

"Probably gone to pick up his Social Security check. He won't be back for two-three days. He always goes on a binge as soon as he cashes his check," Andy said.

"What are we going to do?" George asked.

"Have breakfast," Simon said, picking up the coffee pot. "No point on trying to make a decision on an empty stomach."

"But what if they come back?"

Andy turned and stared at them. He crossed back to the tree and picked up the gun. The blank look was back in his eyes. "Then I'll blow their damned heads off."

Chapter 6

ALTHOUGH THE next two days passed uneventfully, tension lay like a heavy pall over the camp. Andy altered his early warning system and enlarged it but these changes did little to reassure the group.

The weather was no help. Low clouds and misty rain added to the gloom. Simon stayed close to camp, even foregoing his morning runs. The camp was no longer a peaceful haven. Reality had intruded. He wanted to leave, to get on up to Seattle, but couldn't shake the feeling that he would be deserting his new friends. The women were still frightened and jumpy, Billy Joe and George were morose and Andy stalked the camp with the Ak-47 cradled in his arms.

For the first time in years, Simon felt a kinship with someone outside his family. He realized he cared what happened to these people. It was a strange feeling, one he wasn't comfortable with.

Feeling cooped up, frustrated, and mildly resentful, Simon knew he had get away for a while, even if only for a few hours. He needed time alone to sort out these new feelings.

Much of the food had been destroyed by the three loggers and the group was out of milk. It was as good an excuse as any, he decided, as he approached George.

"I'm going to go into town for a few hours, maybe spend the night. I'll bring back some groceries."

All the way down the mountain he thought about the three men who had invaded the camp. Who were they? Frenchie and Stan and a third name he hadn't caught had known where to find them, had know how to avoid Andy's traps. Why was it important to drive them away? So what if they were camped on private land? They were harming no one. They were careful with fire, kept the area clean, and buried their trash.

His intuition, honed by years as a detective, told him there was something going on here. Perhaps if he found out who owned the land it would give him a clue as to why it was so important to drive them out. It wouldn't hurt to do a little checking.

When he got to the highway, he parked on the shoulder and pulled out a map and located the county seat. It wasn't that far. He pulled out and headed south, mentally cursing the drizzle and the gloom.

Windy Creek was a tiny town of less than ten thousand population. It didn't take him long to find the courthouse. He spent the afternoon in the recorder's and assessor's offices making notes.

After leaving the courthouse, he checked into a beach motel and took a hot shower. He found a restaurant noted for its salmon and dined well. Back at the motel, he pulled out the notes he'd made. As near as he could tell without topographical maps, the camp could be located either on property owned by the Goose River Company or in the Siskiyou National Forest. Goose River was owned by another corporation with a Portland address. No individuals were listed on any other records.

He put his notes away and glanced at the phone, then at his watch. It was after eleven o'clock back in Iowa, but his mother always stayed up for the "TONIGHT SHOW".

His brother, Neville, answered with his usual gruff, "Yeah?"

"Hey, Bud, I thought you'd be sawing logs by now. Or aren't you getting up at four anymore to milk the cows?"

"That you, Simon? Where are you?"

"Southern Oregon. How are things back there? How's Mom?"

"Ma's fine, and you know dang well we sold the dairy herd ten years ago. Ain't farming nothing but corn and soybeans."

Simon chuckled. "I know, Bud. I was just pulling your leg. How's Lucille?"

"She's fine."

"And the kids?"

"All fine, too. Here's Ma."

"Simon, is that you?" The soft voice that came over the line conjured up a picture of his mother. A tiny woman with a weather-beaten face under a cloud of white hair. The voice quickened. "How come you're calling so late? Is something wrong?"

"No, Mom, everything's fine. How's everything back there?"

"Just fine, son. Aunt Opal's rheumatism bothered her some this winter but it's a lot better now that the weather's warmed up. Sissy's girl, Mary, just graduated from high school and is working at the co-op this summer to save money for nursing school. How are Orin and Anna Marie?"

"They're both fine. I'll probably see Orin in a week or so."

There was a long pause, then his mother said, "I ain't sure this traipsing around the country like a hobo is such a good idea. Why don't you come on back home if you're tired of California? The farm's still half yours."

"Now, Mom."

"Well, I worry about you. All the stories on the television and in the newspapers. There's a lot of crazies out there. You be careful, you hear!"

"Yes, Mom. I'll call when I get to Orin's in Seattle. You take care of yourself. Night, Mom."

He hung up, chuckling. He was fifty-nine years old and his mother still thought of him as a kid. The last thing in the world he wanted was to go back to the farm. He was sure it was the last thing his brother wanted, too. Neville was the one with an affinity for the land, the one who'd stepped in and taken over when their father had died while Simon had been in Viet Nam.

It was hard to believe that his niece had a girl old enough to graduate from high school. It made him feel old until he remembered that Sissy—
what the hell was his niece's name? He couldn't remember. They'd always called her Sissy. Donna. That was it. Donna. She'd married at fifteen, run off with some hippie. Well, maybe not a hippie, but some no-account boy, and come home a year later with a baby.

Simon stripped down to his shorts and crawled into bed.

When he got to Seattle, he'd call Neville and find out more about the girl. If the kid was serious about going to nursing school, he'd help with the tuition.

It might be nice to go home again for a while. See Mom and Neville. Sit on the wide front porch, in one of the big wicker rockers and smell the honeysuckle that climbed the trellis and blocked the sun. Yes, it might be nice to go home again, at least for a few days. Maybe next spring when the lilacs were in bloom. He drifted off to sleep and dreamed he was a kid again, wading in the creek and digging crawfish out of the mud.

The next morning he drove back to Lion Rock and stopped at the Seaside Cafe for an early lunch. The place was empty. Ruthie was seated at the end of counter with a cup of coffee and the Portland paper. She crushed out a cigarette and stood up as Simon settled at the first table.

"Well, if it isn't the big spender. Where's that cheapskate?"

"If you mean Wheatly, I haven't seen him in a couple of days. What do you recommend for lunch?"

"Special today is lasagna."

"Sounds good. Coffee and some of that apple pie."

When she brought his food, he gestured to a chair. "If you're not too busy, how about joining me?"

"Let me get my coffee."

When she's settled across the table from him, he said, "Tell me a little about Lion Rock."

"Not much to tell. Used to be a prosperous little town until first the fishing and then the lumbering went to hell. Now most of us are just hanging on by our fingernails."

"I'd think you'd get a lot of tourists, at least in the summer."

"Nah. Most of them drive right on through. The beach ain't that great. They either stop at Coos Bay up north or Windy Creek. Nothing here for them to see."

"I'd think the sea lions out on the rocks would attract them."

"Too far away. Can't see much without binoculars."

"I'm surprised no one is running charters out there."

Her eyes widened, then narrowed. "Don't reckon anybody's thought of it, but why not? They run whale-watching boats up the coast. Might not be a bad idea."

"I notice someone seems to be doing okay. That warehouse sorta stands out."

"Oh, that's Avery Tredmore's place."

"Never saw anyone around. What kind of business is he in?"

"Something to do with forest products, I'm not exactly sure what. I heard he'd made a deal with some of the mills for their bark. Seen dump trucks hauling it in. I guess he dries it, bags it and sells it to nurseries and garden supply stores. Pete Wilson was in here complaining about having to cut ferns and collect pine cones."

"Doesn't seem like there'd be much money in that, but then I don't know much about the nursery business."

Ruthie shrugged. They talked of other things while Simon finished his lasagna. As he cut into the pie, he said, "Saw some fellows in here the other day. I think I heard one of them called Stan. Dressed like loggers."

"Stan Lough. Hangs out with Frenchie DuBois and Pete Wilson. Take my advice and stay away from them three. They're bad news. What do you want with them?"

He shrugged. "Somebody said one of them was a good mechanic. I need some body work done on my truck."

"Ha! Somebody must have been pulling your leg. Ain't any of them good for nuthin' except fighting and causing trouble. They'd as likely steal your truck as fix it."

"In that case, maybe you'd better not mention I was asking. I don't want any trouble."

"Ain't a good body man in town since Jerry Gough left. Better take it on up to Coos Bay."

He paid for the meal, left a generous tip and went out. At least he now knew the names of the three men. He still had no idea why they'd attacked the camp.

He started for his truck, then stopped and stroked his jaw. The rain had stopped, the mist had burned away and the sun was shining. It was the most beautiful day since he'd arrived. He didn't really want to go back to camp, at least not yet. It was simply too nice a day to spend in that gloomy atmosphere.

Shoving his hands in his pockets he strolled down the street to the bridge. The tide was in, covering the mud flats. He leaned on the railing and watched seagulls circling and diving and listened to their raucous calls. The two old men were again fishing from one of the piers. Two fishing boats, old and poorly maintained, and a number of skiffs and small pleasure boats bobbed sedately in the wake of an incoming boat.

As Simon watched, the boat throttled back and turned toward the dock next to the one well-maintained warehouse. He admired the way the skipper slid the boat neatly alongside and cut the motor. It was a spiffy boat, rigged for charter fishing. He hadn't been aware that anyone was running charters out of Lion Rock. He'd never been deep-sea fishing. Maybe he'd give it a try before he left. His gaze wandered over the warehouse. Another semi was parked inside the fence. The first one he'd seen had been white; this one was blue.

He strolled back into town and down the hill toward the beach. He passed the hotel and stopped where the pavement ended and the beach began. A row of a dozen or so webbed lounges were lined up in front of the hotel, about half of them occupied. Several sunbathers stretched out on blankets on the sand. Children raced in and out of the water, their shrieks and laughter competing with the cries of the seagulls circling above.

Smiling, Simon sat on the nearest lounge and removed his shoes and socks. He tucked the socks into the toes of the shoes, tied the laces together, and rolling up his pants legs, draped the shoes over his shoulder and ambled toward the water. With the warm sand squishing between his toes, he felt like a kid again.

Halfway down the beach he came across a log half buried in the sand. He sat down on the sand, and leaning back against the log, stared out to sea. The sunlight reflecting off the water made him blink. He wished he'd thought to bring sunglasses. He slipped lower in the warm sand until his head rested against the log and closed his eyes. Between the warm sand and the warmth of the sun, he began to relax. A few minutes later he was sound asleep.

THE SCREAM of a siren penetrated his sleep but by the time he was awake it had stopped and he wasn't sure whether it was real or a part of his dream. Still sleep-logged, he glanced around in momentary confusion, not quite sure where he was. He sat up and tried to rub the stiffness out of his neck. He was too old for this sort of nonsense.

He stood up and started to brush the sand from his clothes when a flashing light farther down the beach caught his eye. As he instinctively started through the sand an ambulance pulled in beside the police car.

Now fully awake, he noticed that the children had stopped playing and were now huddled around their parents. The adults were clustered in several groups staring down the beach.

A couple of the men broke away from one group and walked down the beach. Simon joined them and asked, "What's going on?"

"A body washed up on the beach."

They stopped a few feet away from where the medics were working on the body. Simon had seen his share of floaters and was about to turn away when the medic turned the body over. He froze in a half turn and stared at the bloated face of Buford.

Chapter 7

FRENCHIE DUBOIS stopped inside the door of the LOG JAM and waited a moment, giving his eyes a chance to adjust to the dimness. The bartender was already uncapping a bottle of Bud as he walked toward the bar.

"How ya doing, Frenchie?"

Frenchie merely grunted, grabbed the bottle and took a swig before crossing the room to a back table where Stan Lough and Pete Wilson were seated. Swinging a chair around, he straddled it, hooking his ankles around the legs.

Stan was the first to speak. "So what did the boss have to say?"

"We're to stay away from the mountain for a couple of weeks."

"You shitting us, right?"

"Nope. That's what he said."

"Why? The longer they're up there, the more chance they'll find—"

"Shut up. The boss says leave them alone, we leave them alone."

Pete, who had been making overlapping circles with the bottom of his bottle, looked up and said, "I don't like it. That big fellow was on the bridge watching when I came in this afternoon. I'd like to know who the hell he is."

"Forget it."

"I ain't about to forget it. What if he's a Fed?"

"He ain't no Federal agent."

"How do you know? You see the truck he drives? He ain't no bum, like the rest of them. Did you see that fancy trailer? I say we catch him and work him over, find out what he'd doing up there."

Frenchie finished his beer and slammed the bottle on the

table. "You heard what the boss said. Leave them alone."

"What about that bum that was hanging around the warehouse, the one that told us where to find their camp?"

"Forget him. I paid him off."

"Yeah, but—"

Frenchie stood up. "I got to run down to San Francisco for a few days. Keep out of trouble till I get back."

Pete watched him until the door swung closed behind him, then said, "You think we should have told him?"

Stan took a swig from his beer and shook his head. "Nah. The riptides off that point will have carried him out to sea. He was just a bum. Nobody'll miss him."

"Uh...."

Stan paused, bottle halfway to his lips. "You did throw him off the point, didn't you?"

"Well, uh...not exactly." Pete's voice rose in a nasal whine. "It was too far. What if I'd been stopped? What if..."

"Oh, shit!"

Chapter 8

SIMON TURNED back for a closer look at the body. It was definitely Buford. No matter how many bodies he saw, and he'd seen more than his share, it always clawed at his gut. All of his years of training and experience urged him to step in, identify the body, and offer his help to the local authorities. He fought down the impulse. What could he really tell them? He only knew the one name. Buford. He didn't know whether it had been the man's first or last name or even if it was his real name. Buford had left nothing in the camp so he wasn't withholding evidence. Nothing would be gained by leading the authorities to the camp.

He waited until the body had been taken away, then walked back to the hotel. He needed a drink.

The bar was dark and quiet. He carried his scotch and water to a table in the corner. Buford's death worried him. Remembering the sly look on the man's face the night before he left, Simon had a pretty good idea of how the loggers had found the camp. He wondered how much he'd been paid to rat on the campsite. Did his death have anything to do with whatever was going on up the mountain? What was going on?

He finished his drink and left the bar. Outside he paused and glanced out to sea. A cloudbank hung on the horizon. Damn. It was going to rain again. With a sigh, he turned and walked back up the street. It was time he picked up groceries and headed back to camp.

The first thing he noticed as he drove into camp was Wheat's truck. So the old man was back. He'd missed the old coot!

After giving the groceries to Meg, he went over the where Wheat was working on his truck. Simon leaned on the fender and watched until Wheat finished cleaning and replacing the spark plugs.

"Want to take a walk?" Simon asked.

"I ain't much for walking, les'n I have to," Wheat said, wiping his hands on an already filthy rag.

"A stroll down to the road might do you some good."

Wheat looked up and met Simon's intent gaze. Tossing the rag on the hood, he said, "It might at that."

Simon led the way, crossing the road to the deer path he'd used for his jogs. When they were well away from camp, he stopped and gestured to a couple of stumps. "Might as well take a load off." He glanced around. "This is a pretty spot."

"What is it? You didn't bring me out here to talk about the scenery."

"How well did you know Buford?"

"Not at all. He kept to himself. Why?"

"He's dead." Simon related his nap on the beach and waking to find the police dragging the body in from the surf.

When he finished, Wheat shook his head and said, "He liked his booze. Be just like him to stumble off a pier and drown."

"Maybe. I saw the body. The back of his head had been smashed in."

"Could have hit his head on a piling."

Simon didn't respond. After several minutes, Wheat said, "I wonder where he got the money for the booze. He was broke when he left here."

"I think he was paid for information. I think he told that bunch of goons where to find us. I can't help wondering who else he told. I'm sure I saw him talking to someone at the street fair, and those posters about Meg and Jamie were all over the place."

"Sheee-it! What are we going to do?"

"Nothing we can do but wait and see if someone shows up."

"Think we ought to tell her?"

Simon thought for a moment. "That might not be such a good idea. Meg might try to run. She doesn't have any money. Who knows what kind of trouble they might run into. Here, at least, they have friends. Why don't we wait a few days and see what happens?"

"I guess you're right. We'll keep the whole thing under our hats." He glanced over at Simon. "No need to tell them about Buford either, I reckon. None of them liked him."

As if even the weather welcomed Wheat's return, the rain never materialized and the next morning dawned bright and clear. The despondency that had gripped the camp since the attack evaporated with the moisture. For the next two weeks the sun shone and the atmosphere of the camp warmed along with the temperature. They had no visitors. The garden grew and weeding was an everyday chore. Simon's blisters became calluses. He returned to his morning jogs. Around the campfire at night after dinner, Billy Joe entertained them or they all sang.

An inner peace Simon hadn't know in years crept over him. He knew he should get his truck repaired but he was gripped in inertia, unwilling to interrupt the contentment.

On Tuesday of the third week, the weather changed. Low clouds crept in from the ocean, enveloping the mountain in murky fog. It began a steady drizzle.

On Wednesday night, Simon made a decision that he announced after dinner. "I've got to call my insurance company and get my truck fixed. I'm going up to Portland tomorrow. I'll probably be gone three or four days. Meg, there's still meat in the freezer and you're welcome to use the oven." He handed her the keys to his trailer.

He left early the next morning and drove north. The fog was heavy, making the drive slow until he finally turned east to Corvallis, Albany and Interstate 5. It was mid-afternoon by the time he reached Portland and checked into a motel.

Dumping his gear on the bed, he stripped and went into the bathroom. Catching a glance of himself in the mirror, he shuddered. His hair was much too long and shaggy. He ran a hand over his chin, now covered with a thick, if somewhat ragged beard. He took a long shower, lingering under the spray of hot water.

Wrapped in a bath towel, he called his insurance company who recommended a body shop. He dressed in slightly wrinkled slacks and sport shirt, wiped the dust off his dress shoes, shrugged into a sport coat and left the room.

After locating the body shop that could begin work on his truck the next morning, arranging for a rental car for the two days the shop had estimated it take to complete the repairs, and replenishing his cash from an ATM machine, he found a barbershop.

Hair cut and beard neatly trimmed, he treated himself to steak dinner, picked up an Earl Emerson paperback book and went back to the motel, where he placed a call to his son in Seattle.

They spoke for several minutes and when Simon hung up he had the distinct feeling that Orin was not looking forward to his visit. Something was obviously bothering his son, but it was also obvious that he had no wish to discuss his problems. Oh, well, Simon was no longer in a hurry to get to Seattle. In fact, he was looking forward to getting back to camp and his new friends.

Before he settled down to read himself to sleep, he thought about how he intended to spend the next couple of days. He planned to do a little investigation of the Poindexters.

Simon awoke early, went for a two-mile run, showered and was at the garage by the time they opened. He picked up his rental car, collected another two hundred dollars from another ATM, found a Denny's and ordered a Grand Slam breakfast.

While he waited, he unfolded the city map he'd purchased the night before and took the flier from his pocket. He located the street listed on the flier. Finding the address was not going to be easy. He'd never seen a town with so many hills, rivers and bridges.

When he finally found the street and the house, he was more than a little surprised. Nothing about Meg, her clothes, or the old station wagon, had prepared him for the big white colonial house that perched on the hillside surrounded by a good half acre of landscaping. A drive, bordered on one side by thick shrubbery, curved up the hill. On the other side, a neat edging of pink and white petunias set off by blue lobelia defined the edge of a well-manicured lawn. Across the lawn, Simon saw a white gazebo surrounded by a rose garden in full bloom.

Two vehicles were parked in the wide sweep of gravel in front of the house, a beat-up Ford pickup truck with hand lettering on the side, and an old Chevy. He was too far away to read the lettering on the truck but the tailgate was down and a wooden ramp led up to the bed of the truck. Several garden implements were propped beside the bed of the truck. As Simon watched, a Hispanic man came around the house carrying a large plastic bag and tossed it into the truck.

Simon was debating whether to question the man when a woman with a poodle on a leash walked down the street. The poodle spotted Simon and began yapping. The woman stopped, staring suspiciously at Simon, then at the Ford Escort he was driving. The last thing he needed was someone calling the cops. He opened the city map and spread it across the steering wheel. The woman continued her walk but edged away from car as she came along side. She backed away a couple of steps as he rolled down the window and smiled what he hoped was a reassuring smile.

"Excuse me, but I seem to be lost. Perhaps you can help me. I'm looking for..." He named a similar sounding street that he knew from the map was several blocks away.

She gave him directions and he thanked her. As he drove away, he saw that she was still watching him, still frowning. He turned at the next corner, following her directions, then cut back toward the downtown area.

He found the public library and spent the rest of the morning in the reference section. When he left he knew a little more about Margaret and Wesley Poindexter.

Over lunch, he took out his notebook and re-read the notes he had taken. Margaret Alice Newton and Wesley Alan Poindexter had been married a little over six years previously, the ceremony performed by the bride's father, the Reverend Thomas Newton. Bridesmaids had been a Susan Jean Long and Elizabeth Anne Peters. Poindexter's hometown was listed as Bristol, Connecticut.

Later news stories included the death of Meg's younger brother, James, in a boating accident followed a few months later by the death of her father in an automobile accident. He found the birth announcement for Jamie Lynn. No mention was made in any of the stories of Meg's mother. The most recent news article had been the announcement of Wesley being named a partner in a law firm.

Simon spent the afternoon at the courthouse where he learned that Meg had inherited the house he'd visited that morning from her father, along with a sizable portfolio of blue chips stocks and several pieces of property. When he tracked down the other property, he found that all had been sold in the last three years.

He also looked up Goose River Company and wasn't surprised to see that major stockholder and CEO was Avery Tredmore.

Simon treated himself to dinner at a well-known seafood restaurant, then did something he hadn't done in years. He went to a movie. As he lay in bed that night listening to the sound of traffic on the street, he couldn't stop the questions that raised themselves in his mind. The foremost question was why, with the wealth she'd inherited, was Meg living out of an old Buick station wagon?

After his morning run, shower and breakfast at a nearby restaurant, he went back to the motel, settled himself in a chair next to the telephone and opened the phone book. He called every Long in the book without finding anyone who knew a Susan Long. He had better luck with the list of Peters. On the third call, he reached Elizabeth's mother. He introduced himself as an old acquaintance, without giving his name.

"I was just calling to say hello," Simon said.

"But if you're an old friend, then you know she married last year."

"I've been out of touch since I moved to southern California several years ago."

"Oh, is this Billy Martin? How is your mother? Are you moving back?"

"Mom is fine. No, I'm just passing through and thought I'd touch base with a few old friends."

"California certainly has changed you. You don't even sound like yourself. Elizabeth, indeed. Betty married Jason Denier. I'll tell her you called. Be sure to say hello to your mother for me."

"I will. Thanks, Mrs. Peters."

He located Jason Denier in the phone book and scribbled down the address before dialing. When a young woman answered, he hung up. The name Denier was on the list of attorneys in Poindexter's law firm.

Half an hour later he parked the Escort in front of a modest bungalow on a street of similar homes. The lawn was neatly trimmed with a rose garden in one corner and the house well maintained but hardly what he expected of an up and coming young lawyer in a prestigious law firm.

He rang the bell and waited, admiring the roses. He'd never seen so many roses or such beautiful ones as he'd seen driving around this city. They were everywhere, lush and verdant. No wonder it was called "The Rose City". His gut ached when he remembered how his wife had struggled with the few bushes they'd had in their yard. Hannah would have loved it here where everything seemed to grow in abundance.

The door opened, providing a release from the pain of the past. Betty Denier was a rather plain young woman dressed in jeans and a University of Oregon sweatshirt, her blonde hair pulled back in a ponytail. He'd had several openings planned, but studying Betty Denier's open, intelligent countenance, he rejected them in favor of honesty.

"I'm a friend of Margaret Poindexter. I believe you are, too. May I talk to you for a few minutes?"

Her eyes widened, then narrowed. "Is she all right?"

"At the moment, yes. May I come in?"

She nodded and stepped back. "Let's go in the kitchen. Would you like a cup of coffee?"

"Sure."

When they were seated in an upholstered booth that overlooked the backyard, with coffee cups in front of them, Betty said, "I don't know you. Where did you meet Meg?"

"I'd rather not say."

"How do I know you're really her friend and not working for that bastard?"

"I'm not working for anyone. What bastard are you referring to?"

"Wes. Have you really seen Meg? Is she okay? Why hasn't she gotten in touch with me?"

"Maybe she was afraid. Afraid you'd pass the information on to her husband. You're husband works with him, doesn't he?"

"Jason? No, of course not. Oh, that's his father." Her eyes narrowed again. "Meg didn't tell you that."

"No, Meg hasn't told me anything. Look, let me lay my cards on the table. I met Meg and Jamie a little over a month ago. I don't know what her problem is, but I do know that she's broke, she's terrified, and she needs help. Jamie needs help. I'd like to help them but I can't unless I know what's going on."

"Why do you care? Who are you?"

He pulled out his L.A.P.D. identification. "I'm retired now, taking a long vacation. I won't tell you how or where I met Meg. If she wants you to know, she'll have to tell you herself. But she does need help."

"What do you want to know?"

"Background. You've been friends for a long time? What is she running from? Why is she so frightened?"

"We've been friends since grade school. God, I even introduced her to that bastard, at my father-in-law's annual party for members of the firm. The son-of-a bitch! He had us all fooled with his charm and smooth manners. Well, not everyone. Jason never liked him and I don't think Reverend Newton liked him."

"Did Meg's mother like him?"

"Mrs. Newton died when Jimmy was born."

She stared out the window, idly stirring her coffee. Simon waited patiently for her to continue.

"Mrs. Newton was from an old Portland family. You know, lots of money and prestige. That's why Wes married Meg. He thought...but she only had an allowance and her father stopped that when she got married.

"Meg got pregnant with Jamie and Wes wanted her to have an abortion. When she refused, he beat her up. She almost lost the baby. She left him and went home until the baby was born. I guess her father had a talk with Wes because she went back and he didn't hurt her again, at least not physically, until after her father died."

"She stayed with him?"

"Until a couple of months ago. She...she came by here the morning she left. She had a black eye and a lot a bruises but she'd still have stayed with him except that he'd slapped Jamie around, too. I wanted her to call the cops but she was too afraid of Wes."

"She could have gotten a restraining order."

Betty shook her head. "Wes had her convinced that if she left him, he'd take Jamie. He convinced her that no other lawyer would take her case, that she couldn't win against him."

She reached over and gripped Simon's hand. "Is she really all right? Can you help her?"

"I'm going to try." He stood up. "Thanks for the information and for the coffee."

At the door, she laid a hand on his arm. "Tell her if she wants to come back, she can stay with us. We'll take care of her."

Simon patted her hand. "I'll tell her."

He stopped for a leisurely lunch, turned in the rental car and took a cab back to the motel. He paced the room considering what his next move should be. All cops hated domestic disputes. His gut told him to back away, but he couldn't get Jamie's pathetic little face out of his mind. The child needed help. Meg needed help.

He packed and waited for the call from the garage. It came sooner than expected and by three o'clock he was on his way. Rush hour traffic had already started and coupled with the Friday get-out-of-town crowd made for slow going. Off the Interstate, it was even worse. It seemed to Simon that every camper, motor home and trailer in the western United States was clogging the road.

In Coos Bay he spotted a motel with the VACANCY sign still lit and drove into the parking lot. He got the last room. Too tired to hunt up a restaurant, he got a Coke and chips from the vending machine and made do. He spent a restless night, plagued with nightmares.

Chapter 9

SIMON WAS up before dawn and was on the road before the fog had begun to dissipate. It was slow going at first. The fog eventually melted away, but still Simon didn't hurry. It was going to be a beautiful day and he intended to make the most of it.

The sun was just topping the Coastal Range, gilding the riffles of the ocean with sparkling silver highlights, when he steered the truck into an overlook to enjoy the view. It was as he climbed out of the truck to take a closer look at the surf pounding on the rocks below that he became consciously aware of the red Porsche. It had been behind him all the way from the diner in Coos Bay where he'd stopped for breakfast. The car slowed down as if the driver also intended to drive into the overlook, but as Simon turned to look at it, the car sped away.

He stared after it until it rounded a curve. So the driver had changed his mind. Big deal. Still, the hairs on the back of Simon's neck tickled a message that he was determined to ignore. If he'd still been on the job, Simon would have paid more attention, but he was retired, no longer a cop, and he was on vacation. But the peacefulness of the morning was spoiled. He climbed back in his truck and continued south.

HE SPOTTED the wreckage a few miles north of Lion Rock. He slammed on his brakes and backed to where the shoulder was wide enough to park, a sick dread building in him.

He ran to where the tire tracks had left the road and scrambled down the steep embankment. The scraps of wood littering the ground showed where Wheat's truck had rolled over at least once. The truck lay on its side, the wooden camper shell so smashed it resembled kindling. The truck bed was wrapped around a boulder, the only thing that had prevented it from plunging into the rocks and surf fifty feet below.

Bile rose, burning the back of Simon's throat as he peered in the open door on the driver's side. He fully expected to see Wheat's battered and broken body, but the cab was empty. The shattered, bloodstained windshield was mute evidence that Wheat had not been wearing his seat belt. Had he been thrown from the vehicle? On hands and knees, Simon crept around the boulder and peered down. Nothing.

He moved back and stood up, sucking in deep breaths to calm the churning in his gut. When he'd regained control, he began to look around. From the way the ground was churned with footprints, he obviously was not the first on the scene.

He scrambled back up the steep bank to the highway. Pushing aside his feelings, he surveyed the scene with a critical eye, noting the skid marks and trail of rubber on the pavement. The highway ran straight for several hundred yards in both directions. No curves, no dips, no reason for Wheat to have gone of the highway at this point.

Had the old man fallen asleep at the wheel? No. He'd been awake because he'd ridden his brakes hard and the turn had been too sharp. Had he swerved to avoid something in the road? If so, why to the outside where there was no shoulder? There was plenty of room on the other side. Unless, unless he'd been forced off the road.

Simon returned to his truck and drove slowly toward town. A rage he hadn't felt in years built in his gut. He stopped at the State Patrol office at the edge of town and reported the accident.

The sergeant behind the counter looked like he should have been retired for years and his attitude confirmed it in Simon's mind. "Yeah, happened yesterday. Early in the morning. Some old bum. Probably drunk."

"Where is the body?"

"Huh?"

"His name was Horace Wheatly and he wasn't a bum. Where did they take his body?"

"Oh, he ain't dead...yet. Or he wasn't when they took him to the hospital."

Obtaining directions, Simon drove to the local hospital, and after negotiating his way through the bureaucracy, was finally led to a two-bed room. The second bed was empty.

Wheat lay on his back with the blanket tucked under his chin. Beneath the bandages that wrapped his skull, his face was white and waxy. Though an oxygen tube protruded from his nostrils, the movement of his chest beneath the covers was so slight that for a moment Simon thought the old man had died. His left arm was in a cast.

Simon pulled up a chair and settled down to wait for Wheat to wake. After an hour, he gave up and went in search of the doctor. The man was an East Indian, short and pudgy, with a damp, flabby handshake. It took all of Simon's charm to finally get Dr. Sidhu give him the barest outline of Wheat's condition: massive concussion, ruptured spleen, fractured ribs, broken left arm, multiple abrasions and contusions. The spleen had been removed but the patient remained comatose. Prognosis was guarded. If Wheat regained consciousness, if he did not develop pneumonia or other complications, then they would know more. No, Wheat had not been drunk. Blood tests had shown no signs of alcohol or drugs. When the doctor began inquiring about insurance, Simon beat a hasty retreat.

He drove back to the scene of the accident and clambered down the bank and searched the wreckage. He checked the glove compartment first. It wasn't locked and Simon collected the few papers and stuffed them in his pocket to peruse later. There wasn't much to salvage. He collected what he could: a few items of clothing, a flashlight that still worked, a couple of pans, a couple of dishes that had somehow survived unbroken, a pair of boots and a small metal box, and a woolen army surplus blanket. Bundling everything into the blanket, he climbed back to the highway and stowed the bundle in the back of the camper.

A red Porsche passed heading north as he climbed into the cab. He was sure it was the same one that had followed him from Coos Bay. He drove toward Lion Rock staying just below the speed limit and keeping an eye on the rear view mirror. Just as he entered town, the car appeared in the mirror.

The town was full of tourists. He finally found a parking spot on a side street, locked the truck and strolled back to the

Seaside Cafe. For once, the little cafe was crowded and both Ruthie and a teenage girl were busy waiting on customers.

Simon had to wait several minutes before a stool at the counter became vacant. He glanced at the menu and when Ruthie plunked a glass of water in front of him, he ordered the chicken fried steak. Before she could turn away, he said, "Did you know Horace Wheatly had an accident and is in the hospital?"

She froze, pencil poised above the order pad. "Wheat? When? Are you sure?"

"I was by the hospital a couple of hours ago. He's in a coma."

Before she could respond, a customer called for service and she hurried away. They didn't have another chance to speak until she slid his dinner in front of him.

"How bad is he?" she asked.

"Broken ribs, broken left arm, ruptured spleen, concussion."

"Oh, God."

"Ruthie, who would want to kill that old man?"

"What?"

"He was deliberately run off the road."

She stared at him, eyes widened in shock. "That's not funny. You are joking, aren't you?"

When he didn't respond, she shook her head. "He's just an old rum-pot. Probably drunk."

"No, he hadn't been drinking."

"When did it happen?"

"Early yesterday morning. Did you see him in the last couple of days?"

"No. In fact he hasn't been in since last month." She frowned. "That ain't like him. He's usually in at least once a week trying to cadge a free meal." She paused, then asked, "He's going to be okay, isn't he?"

"According to the doctor, it will depend on when he comes out of the coma. He's in pretty bad shape."

Ruthie went back to work and Simon tackled his dinner. By the time he'd finished, the cafe was nearly empty. Ruthie poured herself a cup of coffee, slid onto the stool next to him and lit a cigarette.

"Have you known Wheat long?" he asked.

"He's been coming in for the last couple of years, but I can't say I know him."

"Do you know if he has any family?"

"He never mentioned any. Fact is, he never did talk much about himself." She snubbed out her cigarette. "He was a crazy old coot, but you know, I liked him. You think it would be all right if I visited him?"

"I don't see why not. I think he'd like it, but you'll have to talk to his doctor. A guy named Sidhu."

When he paid his check, he purchased half a dozen cheap cigars.

It was twilight when Simon left the cafe. He paused on the sidewalk outside and lit a cigar, while he surveyed the street. The red Porsche was parked two blocks away.

He strolled down the street to the bridge and leaned on the railing. The natty cruiser he'd seen come in before was headed out to sea. He watched it until it disappeared as darkness swallowed it up.

Taking his time, he strolled down toward the docks, pausing now and then as if to look at the boats, but actually more interested in seeing if he was being followed. As far as he could tell, he wasn't.

He worked his way back up to his truck and headed out of town. Before he reached the city limits, headlights appeared in his mirror. He didn't know who was following him or why, but he wasn't about to lead them back to the camp. He considered his options. If it was indeed the Porsche, there was no way he could outrun it. What he needed was either a diversion or a way to catch the driver off guard.

The gaudy neon sign of the LOG JAM decided him. He pulled into the parking lot and found a spot between two other pickup trucks with campers. From the shadows of the trucks, he watched the Porsche cruise the lot looking for a parking spot. When the driver did not emerge, Simon stuffed a baseball cap in his jacket pocket and grabbed an old down vest from behind the seat. From the glove box, he took a roll of electrician's tape and tore off a small piece. He opened the door and as he got out, he slapped the tape over the light switch and quickly closed the door.

Wrapping the vest around his waist under his sport coat, he strolled to the door. He paused for a moment under the light to take out another cigar.

Inside he strolled to the bar and ordered a beer. The tavern was crowded with the usual Saturday night crowd of rowdy loggers and fishermen. He stood with his back to the bar where he could watch the door out of the corner of his eye. He'd only taken a couple of sips when the door opened.

Between the crowd of people, the dim lights and the cloud of smoke, it was difficult to get a good look at the man. He had average good looks. His styled blond hair and his gray suede jacket worn over a silk shirt all shouted money. He looked as out of place as a hooker at a revival meeting.

The man's face flushed as the patrons near the door turned to stare at him, several making snide remarks in raucous voices. He glanced around the room. Simon avoided eye contact by turning to the man next to him at the bar and remarking on the fine weather. When he looked back, the man was retreating out the door.

Simon finished his beer and headed for the men's room, where he took off his sport coat, rolled it up and stuffed it inside his shirt adding ten pounds to his silhouette. He rolled up the sleeves of his shirt and put on the vest, then added the baseball cap, pulling the brim low over his forehead.

Leaving the men's room, he slowly circled the dance floor keeping to the shadows while he surveyed the room. The driver of the Porsche had not returned. At the bar, he ordered another beer, took a sip, and clutching the bottle in his hand, headed for the door.

He pushed it open and staggered out, waving the bottle. He weaved his way across the parking lot to the truck on the right of his own. Out of sight of the Porsche, he ducked down and scooted around the front of that truck, eased open his door and slipped inside. A minute later he was driving onto the highway. He headed south, watching his mirror. When no lights appeared, he increased his speed. But just as he reached the turnoff, his relief fled as lights appeared in his mirror.

He cut his lights and took the turn without hitting his brakes. He slid on the gravel, fought for control and raced up the road. He didn't think the maneuver would confuse the driver of the Porsche for long. He'd be sure to back track when he didn't catch up with Simon. There weren't that many side roads along this stretch of highway. But, Simon thought, if he could reach the logging road, there was no way the Porsche could follow him in the dark.

As soon as he had a couple of curves behind him, Simon slowed down and turned on his lights. He sure as hell didn't want to drive off the mountain or miss the logging road.

The camp was quiet as he parked in front of his trailer. Only a few embers glowed in the fire ring. He got out and hesitated, debating on whether to wake someone or wait until morning. As he stood undecided, Andy stepped out of the shadows, the automatic weapon cradled in his arms. Didn't the man ever sleep?

At least Simon's decision had been made for him. He walked over to the fire pit and motioned for Andy to join him. Stirring up the coals, he threw on a couple of sticks and sat down on a stump. Andy shook the coffee pot and set it closer to the fire.

"Did you hear about Wheat?" Simon asked as Andy settled himself on the next stump.

"He ain't back, yet, if that's what you mean."

"He's in the hospital. Someone ran him off the road."

Andy didn't respond for several seconds, and when he did it was one word. "Who?" It was the tone that sent shivers up Simon's spine.

"I don't know. He's in a coma. Maybe he can tell us if...when he comes out of it."

He waited while Andy digested that before continuing, "Someone followed me from Coos Bay today. A red Porsche. I didn't get a good look at the driver, but he's about six feet tall, a hundred and seventy pounds, blond hair. I ditched him for tonight, but he's sure to find the gravel road tomorrow. By the way, where does it go?"

"About thirty miles to Lake Hammond."

"Is that a town?"

"Nope. Used to be, but there ain't nothing left but a couple of foundations."

"He might find where I turned off."

Andy nodded and stood up. "I'll take care of it at first light."

Simon sat, staring into the fire, for a long time after Andy vanished into the shadows. The stress and the emotional upheaval of the day had left him exhausted. He wondered if he had the strength left to walk across the clearing to his trailer. He thought he'd left the violence behind him. He was too old for this! In a few months he'd be sixty. He suddenly felt every one of those years.

Admit it. He was *old*. An old man. A tired old man. A lonely old man. God, how he missed Hannah. These were the years they'd looked forward to, the so-called golden years. Retired, the kids gone, *their* years. The plans they'd made. *Oh, God, Hannah, I need you!*

He wiped away the tears that were streaming down his cheeks and stumbled his way to the trailer. He fell onto the bed without bothering to undress. Maybe tomorrow would be better, maybe not. He cried himself to sleep.

Chapter 10

SIMON SLEPT long and deep and awoke lethargic and woolyheaded. He stripped and pulled on a set of sweats, grabbed a towel and headed for creek. He kept his head down and managed to avoid eye contact with the others. He was in no shape for conversation. Not yet. What he had to tell them would require concentration and tact and for that he'd need a clear head.

Using Andy's technique, he entered the water in a shallow dive and came up sputtering. The water hadn't warmed more than a degree in the month he'd been here. He paddled around the pool several times until the exercise and cold got his blood to flowing and cleared his head. By the time he climbed out, he felt more like his normal self. He was able to put the past night's maudlin bout of self-pity behind him. An aberration, that's all it had been. A momentary weakness. There would be no more of *that!* Hannah would have been ashamed of him.

He strode back to camp. All but Andy were gathered around the fire ring as he approached. Meg handed him a mug of coffee as he took a seat on a stump. They were all silently watching him, waiting.

George broke the silence. "I see you got your truck fixed."

Simon nodded. "Did Andy tell you about Wheat?"

"That he'd had an accident? Yeah."

"That all?"

"That he's in the hospital."

Simon recounted his finding of the wreck and his visit to the hospital. He didn't mention the red Porsche.

There was a long silence as they digested his words and Simon finished his coffee. Meg was the first to speak. "Do you think we should go in and visit him?"

"No!" The word came out sharper than he'd intended. He lowered his voice. "No, not yet. Wheat's in a coma so it wouldn't do any good."

Lovey had been watching him intently and now said, "There's more that you aren't telling us. I think we have the right to know everything."

Simon studied their faces. Lovey was right; they had a right to know. Everything. He sighed.

"Okay. A lot of what I am going to say is supposition, but it's based on my experience as a homicide detective."

There was general in-taking of breath. Meg's face turned so white he was afraid she was going to faint. Billy Joe's muttered, "You're a cop?", and the tightening of the other faces weren't lost on him. The air was suddenly thick with tension and hostility. Only Lovey seemed to regard him without revulsion.

George was glaring at him as he said, "You lied to us. You came up here to spy on us."

"No. I am retired," Simon said. "I'm doing exactly what I said I was, seeing the country. But there is something going on up here."

Billy Joe sprang up. "Bull shit! You're trying to pin something on us."

"No, I'm not! Do you want to hear what I know and what I think? If so, just sit down and listen."

It was Lovey who said in a calm voice, "Sit down, Billy. I think we should listen to what he has to say. Go ahead, Mr. Threadneedle."

"First, let me say that I think you're all good people."

"Gee, thanks a lot," Billy Joe muttered.

Simon ignored him. "But I think you're in the middle of something that you don't even know about. What I don't know. Did Wheat tell you about Buford?"

There was a general shaking of heads. "What about him," George asked.

"He's dead. His body was found on the beach in Lion Rock. I think he was murdered."

Simon watched their reaction, but saw nothing but shock and disbelief of their faces. "Have any of you seen him or talked to him since he left here?" They shook their heads, almost in unison. At least he now had their full attention. He continued, "I saw him at a distance at the street fair."

He paused then asked, "Didn't you wonder how those loggers found us? How they came straight in here without setting off any of Andy's alarms?"

Billy Joe was the first to respond. "You think he told them?"

"Why would he do it?" Frannie asked. "He was staying here, too."

"But he never came back after that weekend," George said.

"My guess is he did it for money," Simon said. "I don't think that's the only information he was trying to sell. Lovey, do you still have a copy of that flyer?"

She nodded. "Want me to get it?"

"Yes."

They sat in silence until she returned. Simon motioned for her to give it to Meg. The young woman read it twice, and when she looked up, her face was haggard but her eyes flashed. "You knew about this? All of you? Why didn't you tell me?"

Frannie went over and put an arm around the girl. "We were afraid you'd cut and run, honey. We thought you'd be safer here with us, where you have friends who could protect you."

"No." She glanced frantically around the clearing. "No, we've got to go. Now. We've... we've—"

"I think you should stay here, Meg," Simon said, "But I have to tell you that I think Buford called your husband."

Meg jumped up and looked around in desperation. Jamie, who had been crouching at Meg's knee, looked up. Her eyes were wide with fear. She clutched at Meg's leg.

"Sit down, Meg," Simon said. "I don't think Buford told him where to find you. I think he was holding out for the reward. But your husband does know you're in this area. I think Buford also told him something about the rest of us, too. Right now, I'm sure he doesn't know where we are. He may be waiting for you to run or for one of us to lead him to you."

He waited for his words to sink in, then asked, "Does you husband drive a red Porsche?"

"Yes. How did you know?"

"Is he about six feet with blond hair?"

"Oh, God, you talked to him. That's why you went to Portland!"

"No, I didn't talk to him. I did see your friend, Betty, and she told me about your problems. I think he followed me from Coos Bay yesterday. I lost him last night, at least temporarily."

"Do you think he killed Buford?" George asked.

"Possibly, but I doubt it. What I am sure of is that someone deliberately ran Wheat off the road. If his truck hadn't hung up on a boulder, it would have plummeted all the way into the ocean. If the wreck hadn't killed him, he'd have drowned. Chances are his body would have washed out to sea and never been found. As it is, he's lucky to be alive."

"But who would want to kill Wheat?" Frannie asked in a shaken voice. "He never hurt anyone."

Simon shrugged. "Maybe he can tell us if...when he comes out of his coma."

They were all silent for several minutes, then George asked, "What should we do?"

"For now, I suggest we do nothing. I picked up a cellular phone while I was in Portland. We can call the hospital a couple of times a day to check on Wheat. Do we have enough food to last for a few days?"

At Meg's nod, he continued. "This place isn't that easy to find. If no one leaves, they can't be followed. I think we should all just sit tight for a few days. He may decide Buford was lying to get the reward and go back to Portland."

"And if he doesn't?" Billy Joe asked angrily.

"Then we'll deal with that problem when it arises."

Billy Joe jumped up and began to pace. "I got a gig at the LOG JAM next week. I need the money."

Simon shrugged. "Your decision." He emptied the dregs of his coffee and stood up, glancing around the group. No one met his eyes. With an inward sigh, he walked back to his trailer. The weight of their hostility and suspicion depressed him, but there wasn't much he could do about it.

He sank down on the dinette bench. When had the police become the enemy? When he was a kid growing up back in Iowa, a policeman was regarded as a friend, someone respected, someone to turn to in time of trouble. Now the "pigs" were the enemy, to be avoided, feared.

Resentment churned in him. What the hell, he'd tried. If they couldn't accept him, then it was time he moved on. He was retired. Whatever was going on was none of his business. Let the local cops worry about it. Tomorrow he'd hitch up and head on north.

A tap on the door interrupted his thoughts. Reluctantly, he called, "Come on in."

The whole trailer seemed to tilt as Lovey hoisted her bulk through the door. Simon started to stand up. Lovey waved him back with a smile, leaned against the kitchen counter, and said, "Don't let them get you down. They'll get over the shock."

"Whatever."

"You're thinking of pulling out. Don't do it. We need you."

"Yeah, right."

"Your feelings are hurt. So what? You're a big boy. You can handle it. You were suspicious of us when you first arrived."

Simon started to speak but Lovey raised a hand and said, "Don't deny it. You slept with a gun in your hand that whole first night."

Simon's eyebrows shot up. "How do you know?"

Lovey chuckled. "Madam Zura knows everything."

Almost against his will Simon found himself smiling. "Everything, huh? So tell me, what's going on around here?"

Lovey's smile faded. "I don't know, but whatever it is, it's bad. There is an evil presence hanging over this mountain. So far, it hasn't bothered us, but now...." Her face settled into grim lines making her look suddenly old and vulnerable. " Something bad is going to happen. Soon. I can feel it even if I can't see it."

Simon shifted uncomfortably. "Look, I really am retired. You'd be better off talking to the local authorities."

Lovey shook her head. "To them we're just a bunch of squatters. We need you. Don't run away because your feelings are hurt. Please stay."

He knew Lovey was right. In his years as a cop he'd become inured to the distrust and resentment of a major segment of the population. He'd learned not to take it personally. But this *was* personal and it had hurt. He sighed and looked at her.

"I doubt if there is much I can do but I'll hang around a few more days."

Lovey gave him a singularly sweet smile as she opened the door. "You're a good man, Simon Threadneedle."

"Oh, sure. Sweet talk works every time." He gave her a lopsided grin.

THERE WAS an uncomfortable tension in the camp the next day. Simon stayed in his trailer, going out only to report on his phone calls to the hospital. Wheat remained in a coma. The only good news was that his other injuries were healing, and so far, the dreaded pneumonia had not appeared.

It tore at his heart to watch Meg drag around the camp, her brow creased with worry, her eyes fearful. She jumped at every unusual sound and couldn't hide her fear from Jamie. The child grew even more withdrawn; her eyes, too, were haunted.

The tension and suspicion gradually eased but the days dragged for Simon. The Fourth of July was approaching. Lovey, George and Frannie needed money and couldn't afford to miss the annual celebration. And Billy Joe...at least there was something he could do for the boy. Maybe.

Digging out his address book, he dialed a Hollywood number. Marty Feinberg came on the line with a boisterous, "Simon, you gonif, how the hell are you?"

"Fine, Marty."

"I heard you got the shit shot out of you."

"A year ago."

"Well, hey, let's do lunch. What day's good? For you, all my days are clear. Tomorrow?"

Simon laughed. "That would be difficult. I'm up in Oregon. Listen, I need to ask a favor."

"Hey, for you, anything. Hadn't a been for you, my Shelly—"

"Yeah, well, there's a boy up here—"

"What! You into boychicks, now? I don't believe it."

"Knock it off, Marty. This kid is a blue grass, I think that's what they call it, singer. He's good. Great voice but it's something else, something more. Remember how the kids used to mob the Beatles? Well, this kid has grown women going crazy the same way."

"No shit! So who is this wunderkinder?"

"His name is Billy Joe Johnson."

"Never heard of him."

"He's young. About nineteen, I'd guess. But he's good, Marty, really good."

"So what do you want me to do?"

"Come on, Marty. I want to send him down to you. I want you to see what you can do for him."

"Simon, you got any idea how many young wannabe's there are in this town. Shit."

"Will you just listen to him?"

There was a long pause. Finally Feinberg said, "Sure, Simon. For you I'll listen. If he really is any good, I'll see what I can do."

"Thanks. I'll send him down."

"Whatever."

Simon hung up. Now, all he had to do was convince Billy Joe that he wasn't the enemy. He hunted up a box of stationery and sat down to compose a letter of introduction. That done, he opened the door and surveyed the camp. Billy Joe was nowhere in sight. Frannie looked up from her worktable and Simon called across, "When you see Billy Joe, ask him to come over."

At Frannie's nod, he retreated into the kitchen. He had a fresh pot of coffee going and bacon frying when Billy Joe tapped on the side of the trailer, then sidled in. He gave Simon a tentative smile, but his body language told a different story. He was as tense and wary as a wild animal.

"Have a seat. Coffee's almost done. I don't know about you, but I'm hungry as hell."

Billy Joe slid onto the bench without speaking as Simon forked the bacon onto a paper towel and cracked four eggs into the grease. He poured two mugs of coffee and put them on the table. Out of the corner of his eye, he saw Billy Joe slowly relax and reach for a mug.

When they finished eating, Simon stacked the dishes in the

sink, poured them each more coffee and slid the letter across the table. He waited patiently while Billy Joe read. When the boy raised his head and looked at Simon questioningly, he said, "Marty Feinberg is one of the top agents in Hollywood. He handles people like Kenny Morgan. I talked to him this morning. He's willing to listen to you. Will your gig at the LOG JAM give you enough money to get to Los Angeles?"

"Yes, but why are you doing this? I mean...."

Simon shrugged. "I've heard you sing."

"But—"

"No buts. Just make the most of this chance." He stood up, collected the cellular phone, and went out, saying over his shoulder, "Now, I need to talk to Lovey. I'll see you later."

Chapter 11

WHILE SIMON had been waiting for Billy Joe, he'd come to the decision that he could do his friends more good away from camp. He might be retired and have no official standing but he still had years of experience in investigating. He had a pretty damned good idea of what was going on up the mountain. Those loggers had found a new way to earn a living, a new crop to harvest. Marijuana. The idea that they were making a good living out of decorative bark and ferns just didn't make sense. Those nocturnal trips up the mountain couldn't supply a couple of semi's full of ferns.

Andy knew all about it. The man spent too much time in the woods not to have scouted out the "farm". Lovey, too. She'd certainly dropped enough hints. Wheat had known. Was that why he'd been run off the road? He was also sure that none of the group were involved in any way.

He could, of course, report his suspicions to the local authorities. But all he had was suspicion. No facts. No evidence. Besides, his gut told him there was more involved than a few marijuana plants.

The answers weren't here on the mountain. Also, in town, he'd maybe find a way to side-track Meg's husband. Leaving the cell phone with Lovey, and telling her he'd see the rest of the group at the Fourth of July celebration, he headed down the mountain.

Like an old fire horse smelling smoke, Simon felt himself come alive.

He checked into the Seaside Motel paying a week in advance, put away the few clothes he'd brought with him and got back in his truck. He cruised through town but saw no sign of the red Porsche.

He drove to the hospital. There had been no change in the

old man's condition. He'd read somewhere that coma patients were often aware of their surroundings, even though they couldn't respond. He spent an hour sitting beside Wheat telling him that things were going well at the camp, how fast the garden was growing, about Billy Joe going to Hollywood after the celebration, urging the old man to get well. Simon told Wheat about salvaging what he could from the truck and thought he saw one eyelid twitch. Simon's heart flipped and he kept talking, watching the lined face expectantly, but when there was no further reaction, he decided he'd probably imagined that tiny response.

Leaving the hospital, he cruised back up town but there was still no sign of the red Porsche until he pulled into the motel parking lot. The Porsche was parked three rooms down. The curtain twitched as he parked.

He collected his fishing gear and strolled down to the river, fighting the urge to look over his shoulder. The two old men were again fishing from the dock.

"Anything biting?" he asked as he began to rig his line. He glanced back at the street and swallowed a grin as the Porsche driver hurried down the street, then slowed and began to stroll as he spotted Simon. The man took a seat on a piling at the end of the dock and pulled out a pipe.

"Nope, ain't caught nothing yet," the more garrulous of the two old men replied, eyeing Simon's gear. "What you figure on using for bait?"

"Got this lure that's supposed to be irresistible."

"Sucker born every minute," the other man said.

"Don't pay him no mind. He likes cut herring for bait. Now me, I like clam necks."

"My name's Simon Threadneedle. Mind if I join you?"

"It's a free country. Or so they say. Pull up a bucket. I'm Jim Thorne and this here friendly cuss is Bob Landry."

Landry harrumphed, spit and snapped, "If you don't stop jabbering, you'll drive all the fish away."

For a half an hour or so, they fished in silence. Nothing was biting, but that didn't detract from the enjoyment.

Without appearing to, Simon kept an eye on the pipe

smoker. The man was obviously unused to the relaxed contemplation of nature. Within a few minutes, he began to fidget.

From the end of the pier, Simon had a good view of the waterfront. He noticed the boat tied up at the next pier. It was the same boat he'd seen days before. This time it rode low in the water. He turned to Thorne. "That's a sharp looking boat. Who's the owner?"

"Avery Tredmore."

Landry growled, "Why you so interested?" He eyed Simon coldly.

"I'd like to do some deep sea fishing. Is his office in that warehouse?"

"Ha! Tredmore don't take out no charters, leastways not that I've ever seen. Only ones ever take that boat out are those no-accounts he's got working for him," Thorne said.

"You'd best keep your tongue between your teeth, you old fool," Landry snapped.

"I'll say what I please, knucklehead."

Simon eyed the warehouse thoughtfully as the two old men continued to argue and hurl insults at each other.

After a while, his stomach grumbled. He was surprised to see it was nearly five o'clock. He reeled in his line, put away his lure and broke down his rod.

"Ain't quitting already, are you?" Thorne asked.

"My belly's beginning to think my throat's been cut." As Simon gathered his tackle, he noticed the door to the Avery warehouse open, but no one came out. Carrying his gear, he ambled up the pier and turned into the street. Watching the warehouse door out of the corner of his eye, he thought he saw the silhouette of a man but couldn't be sure. He'd only gone a few paces past the piling where Poindexter was seated when a heavy hand clamped on his shoulder. He stopped, shaking off the hand, and turned.

"Where are my wife and daughter?"

Simon raised an eyebrow. "Do I know you?"

Poindexter moved in close to Simon, trying to intimidate him by invading his space. Since Simon topped Poindexter by a good three inches and outweighed him by 30 pounds, it didn't work.

He tried bluster instead. "Don't give me that shit. I'm Wes Poindexter. You were watching my house. Paula Massey called me. She thought you were planning to rob the place and took down your license number. I had one of our investigators check you out. He followed you when you went to see Betty Denier and when you picked up your truck. Where are Margaret and Jamie? Tell me where they are, you bastard."

When Simon didn't answer, Poindexter threw a punch aimed at Simon's chin. Hands full of fishing gear, Simon reacted by swaying to the side and turning on the balls of his feet. The punch sailed harmlessly over his shoulder. Simon kicked out, catching Poindexter behind the right knee. Already off balance, the attorney collapsed on the pavement. Simon marched on up the street toward the motel, leaving the frustrated man hurling curses and threats at his back.

After showering and changing, Simon left his room and drove out of town to the steak house. Replete and relaxed after a good meal, he drove to the hospital and spent an hour at the side of Wheat's bed.

There was no sign of Poindexter or the Porsche when he got back to the motel. He called Lovey, reported on Wheat and learned that everything was normal at the camp. He went to sleep reading Dana Stabenow's book, *Break up*, set in Alaska and featuring Kate Shugak. He was fascinated by the descriptions of the land and people. Perhaps after his visit with Orin, he'd head up to Alaska.

He awoke out of a nightmare; sweating, heart racing, adrenaline flowing. It wasn't the first time he'd relived the shooting in his dreams but it always left him shaken and depressed.

He turned on the light and looked at his watch: 3:05. He rolled over and tried to go back to sleep, but after a few minutes, he knew it was hopeless. He got up and dressed. Perhaps a walk would calm him.

The red Porsche was again parked in the lot. Simon walked up to the street, sucking in great gulps of the cool, moisture-laden air. Wisps of fog floated on the still air. The little town was silent, only the amorphous glow of an occasional streetlight pierced the darkness. He began to relax, his jangled nerves soothed by quiet of the night. He rambled all the way to the middle of the bridge. He lit a cigar and leaned on the railing. Here the fog was so thick he couldn't see the water. He caught a flicker of movement. Some one else who couldn't sleep? An animal scavenging? Tossing away the cigar, he turned back. As he left the bridge he had the uneasy feeling that he was being watched. He walked slowly, straining to pick any sound. Twice he thought he heard footsteps.

A strident curse shattered the night. Simon stopped. The last thing he wanted or needed was to run into a quarrelsome drunk or have another set-to with Poindexter. He waited, but the sound wasn't repeated. He moved on, walking slowly, turned the corner and came to an abrupt stop.

Below him was the Tredmore warehouse. A semi was pulled up to the loading dock. Men scurried back and forth between the warehouse door and the trailer. Simon couldn't see what they were loading. He stepped into the deeper shadows beside a building and watched, every instinct quivering like a bird dog on point.

Hunched down and keeping to the shadows, he inched his way to a clump of bushes that crowded against the chain link fence. Blackberries! They tore at his face and hands as he tried to push his way through. He finally gave up and crawled back to the shadow of the building.

A few minutes later, four men came out of the warehouse and stood in conversation for a brief moment before two returned to the warehouse. A third climbed into the semi and started the motor. Simon got a good look at the fourth man as he came to the fence to open the gate. Frenchie DuBois. When the truck passed through the gate, Simon recognized the driver, Stan Lough. When the truck reached the corner, the headlights and running lights came on and Simon read the license number. The truck headed south. Simon mentally filed away the license number and turned his attention back to the warehouse.

He watched Frenchie walk back into the warehouse leaving

the gate unlocked and open. Simon was considering slipping inside when the warehouse door opened again. Someone dropped off the far side of loading dock and a moment later a black Cadillac pulled out from the shadows, purred across the parking lot and out the gate. The car's windows were tinted and it was too dark for Simon to read the license plate. Before Simon could decide on his next move, Frenchie was back closing and locking the gate.

Simon stayed in the shadows for another few minutes, but there was no further activity. He walked slowly back to the motel, keeping to the shadows and running what he'd seen through his mind.

Back in his room, he dug out his address book and picked up the phone.

After several rings, a gruff voice barked, "Yeah?"

"My, aren't you a ray of sunshine this beautiful morning."

"Simon?" A series of clanks and clunks and a muttered curse came across the wire. "Shit, man, do you know what time it is? It's four fucking thirty in the morning!"

"Just thought you being a hotshot CHP bigwig, now, you'd like knowing a semi loaded with drugs is headed your way."

There was a moment of silence, then the voice on the end began shooting crisp questions. Simon told his friend everything he suspected, describing the truck and giving him the license number.

"So what you're saying is this truck may or may not be carrying drugs."

"That's right, Mel, but I thought you might like the heads-up."

"Okay, we'll take it from here. And, hey, thanks for the tip. Give me your number and I'll call you back if it pans out."

Chapter 12

SIMON SLEPT late. He saw the curtain in Poindexter's unit twitch as he got in his truck. The red Porsche followed him to the cafe and parked down the block. Using Ruthie's phone, Simon called Lovey.

"I'm going to lead Poindexter out of the area for a few hours. If any of you need to go town, do it now, but don't let Meg leave and don't take too long in town."

After a hearty breakfast he headed south, smiling as he saw the Porsche on his tail. In Bandon, he strolled around, looking in shop windows, stopping in a sporting goods store to look at fishing tackle, but keeping an eye on Poindexter. The attorney, obviously getting bored, ducked into a coffee shop and took a seat in the window where he could see Simon's truck.

Simon continued to walk around town until Poindexter left the cafe. When he was sure the attorney was watching him, he made a point of looking at his watch, then increased his pace. He hurried down the north jetty that, with its sister jetty six hundred feet to the south, protected the harbor. At the tip of the jetty stood the Coquille River Lighthouse.

Already a number of tourists waited for the park ranger to begin a tour. Craning his neck as if looking for someone, Simon worked his way into the group. A glance over his shoulder showed Poindexter studiously looking at the riprap that supported the jetty. He was still intent on the huge boulders when the tour ended. Simon hung back, talking to the ranger, as the rest of the tourists straggled down the jetty.

Simon felt like laughing aloud as Poindexter stomped after the last of the tourists. Thanking the ranger, Simon walked leisurely back to his truck. The red Porsche was nowhere in sight as he drove north. He stopped to hike along Whiskey Run Beach, famous for booze smuggling during prohibition.

It was dusk when he got back to Lion Rock and stopped at the Seaside Cafe. Hunger was burning a hole in his gut. He took a table in the window of the empty cafe and smiled as Ruthie slapped down a menu and a glass of water.

"We're about to close but I guess we can fix you something. Seen Wheat today?" she asked.

"Not yet. Plan to go to the hospital as soon as I've eaten. What's good today?'

"Huh! You better have the chicken fried steak."

He handed back the menu without looking at it. "Sounds good."

"Coffee and pie?"

"Sure."

When she brought his meal, she sat down across from him and lit a cigarette. "You know that idea you had about taking tourists out to see the sea lions? Well, I told Gude Gustafson and that old fool has got his grandkids scraping down that old boat of his. He's going to paint her up fancy and give it a try."

"Why does that make him a fool? I think it's a good idea."

Ruthie chuckled. "Don't guess you've ever been on a working fishing boat. They ain't never gonna get the stink of fish off that old scow."

"Maybe that will just add ambience to the cruise."

"Maybe. If it don't have them landlubbers heaving their guts out before they ever get out of the harbor."

"Well, I wish him luck."

"I suppose it might work. Ellie, that's his granddaughter, was in here today with a bunch of books from the library. Says she's studying up so she can be the tour guide."

She stubbed out her cigarette and lit another one as Simon started eating the pie. "Somebody in here earlier wanting to know where you was staying. City fellow."

"What did you tell him?"

"Told him I didn't know."

"Thanks, Ruthie."

"No thanks needed. I just told the truth. Guessing ain't knowing."

It was full dark by the time Simon left the cafe. As he

strolled up the street toward his truck, the pickup he's seen on the mountain passed him. He paused, watching the taillights. Then, farther down the block, the red Porsche pulled out and drove in the same direction.

He spent an hour at Wheat's bedside and afterwards drove to the motel. No red Porsche stood in the parking lot and Poindexter's unit was dark.

The message light on the phone was blinking. The first message was from Lovey saying that George, Frannie and Billy Joe had gone to town but that the truck had broken down. George and Frannie were staying at the motel in unit twelve and Billy Joe was going to sleep on the beach. Could Simon drive them up the mountain?

The second was a message to call his friend, Mel Hammick, and the number listed was his office. When Mel came on the line, Simon asked, "Working kind of late for such a big shot, aren't you?"

"Yeah, thanks to you."

"Did you catch the truck?"

"Oh, yeah. Got a drug dog out at the weigh station just in time." He paused.

Simon gritted his teeth. "So, are you going to tell me or not? Did you find anything?"

"Yeah. We found bags of cedar bark, bundles of ferns and boxes of pine cones."

"That's all?"

"Not exactly. Underneath all that shit was a bale of high-grade marijuana and almost a ton of Asian heroine. Uncut."

Simon whistled. "A ton?"

"Well, not really, but it was a hell of a haul. Biggest I've ever seen." Mel laughed. "We've contacted DEA and I imagine there'll be some action up in your neck of the woods before long."

"You did keep me out of it, didn't you?"

"Oh, yeah. We were just doing one of our usual spot checks when we came across it. You know we CHiPies are always on the ball."

"Has the driver said anything?"

"Nah, he clammed up as soon as we put the cuffs on him. But he's sweating."

"Good luck."

"You going to be at this number if I need to talk to you again?"

"For a few more days. Then I'll probably be heading on up the coast."

"Keep in touch."

Filled with a deep sense of satisfaction, Simon slept the sleep of the just.

Billy Joe was leaning against the front fender of his truck when Simon came out the next morning. He cast a quick glance across the parking lot, but the space in front of Poindexter's unit was empty.

"Lovey said to ask you if you'd take us up the mountain this morning," Billy Joe said. "They need the groceries and it's going to take a couple of days to get George's truck fixed."

"Sure. Where are George and Frannie?"

"I'll get them."

He trotted down the walk. Simon unlocked his truck and opened the camper shell. They loaded the groceries in the back.

"I don't know about you, but I need some breakfast. My treat."

While they ate, Simon kept his eyes peeled for the red Porsche. He continued to kept watch as they started up the mountain, but no one followed them. As they came on the sharpest blind curve, Simon hit the brakes.

Frannie, sitting in seat beside him, gasped. "What's the matter? What's wrong?"

Simon threw the truck in park and scrambled out. George and Billy Joe climbed down from the back of camper and followed Simon up the road. Deep, rutted skid marks in the gravel led to crushed bushes at the edge of the road.

The three men stood in silence gazing down at the crushed red car three hundred feet below.

Chapter 13

FANNIE'S CHOKED, "Oh, my God," shook them out of their stunned silence.

"Reckon there's anyone alive down there?" Billy Joe asked.

"We'd better find out." Simon started to work his way down the steep slope. About forty feet down, he found Poindexter's body. The man was dead.

Simon scrambled back up to the road. "It's Meg's husband."

"Oh, my God. Is he...?"

"Yes. We've got to report this to the Sheriff's office. We'll go on up to the camp and use the cell phone. Frannie, can you break it to Meg? I'll come back and meet with the officers."

They drove in silence the rest of the way. Frannie took Meg aside while Simon told the rest of the group. When Simon had used the cell phone to call, Lovey asked, "Do you think they'll decide Meg had something to do with it?"

Without a word, Andy picked up his AK47 and disappeared into the woods.

"Was she here with you last night?"

"I guess so. We all went to bed pretty early, but we'd have heard if she'd driven out."

"Then I don't think she has anything to worry about. I've got to get back down the hill."

"I'll go with you," George said.

On the drive down, George said, "I guess we'll all have to move on now. Billy Joe said you'd set something up for him in L.A. Maybe Frannie and me'll just head on south with him as soon as the truck gets fixed." He sighed. "Sure am going to miss this place. You think Meg and Jamie'll be able to go home now?"

"Yes."

They waited at the accident site nearly an hour before Deputy Cass Owens showed up. It was mid afternoon before the body had been removed, the car hoisted up the cliff and hauled away, and the immediate investigation completed.

A SOMBER group gathered around the cold ashes of the campfire when Simon drove in, followed by the sheriff's cruiser. A quick glance showed Simon that every trace of Andy's camp had been cleared and the veteran was nowhere to be seen.

There was a new member in the group. An old man, shriveled and so dirty it was difficult to tell the color of his clothes, glanced up, then back down at his bare feet. Long, gray hair hung down his back in a tangle that looked like it hadn't been washed or combed in years. His gray beard, reaching almost to his waist, was equally dirty.

Billy Joe spoke first. "This here is Jacob. He's got something to tell the sheriff. Go on, Jacob."

The old man's voice was dry and scratchy as he said, "It was them two what done it."

Owens pulled out his notebook and squatted next to the old man. "What's your name?"

"Jacob"

"Jacob what?"

"Doan remember. Jist Jacob."

"Where do you live?"

The old man's head came up, a look of pure panic in his eyes. "Ain't sayin'. Ain't nobody's business."

Billy Joe spoke up. "Jacob's a hermit. Lives somewhere up on the mountain."

"Well, Jacob, what exactly did you see?"

"It was them two, the one's growing them bushes on up the mountain. Seen 'em plenty of times. Big black truck. They stopped crosswise the road just around that curve. That little car had no place to go 'cept over the edge. Them two got outa the truck and looked over and laughed, then they got back in and drove on up the mountain. Did it on purpose, they did."

"Frenchie DuBois and Pete Wilson. I saw Poindexter follow them out of town last night," Simon said.

Owens asked more questions, then closed his notebook and stood. He looked at Jacob. "Can you show me where they are growing those bushes?"

Jacob glanced around the group. "Do I gotta?"

When no one answered, he got stiffly to his feet and shuffled after Owens to the cruiser.

It was George who asked, "You going to chase us out of here?"

Owens glanced around the campsite and shrugged. "Not my land. Depends on what Avery Tredmore wants done. But I think he's going to be too busy with other problems to worry about it for a while."

As they watched the cruiser leave, Frannie said, "I wonder what he meant by that."

Simon smiled, but didn't respond. He glanced around, "Where's Andy?"

"He's around. He went out and found Jacob and brought him here, but he don't like anyone in uniform. He'll be back once things quiet down."

Simon thought for a moment, then said, "I'm going back to town. I think it would be best if you all just stayed here for a while. Nothing to be gained by rushing off willy-nilly. I don't think anyone is going to bother you." He handed the cell phone back to Lovey. "I want to check on Wheat and see what's going on in town. I'll keep in touch."

IN TOWN, he slowed at the corner and watched the activity at Tredmore's warehouse. The parking lot was filled with cars. Men in dark jackets, the white DEA letters clearly visible, swarmed in and out of the building and over the boat. Owens had been right. Avery Tredmore had more to worry about than a few squatters.

Simon drove on to the hospital. As he entered, the receptionist hailed him. "The doctor has been trying to reach you. Are you going to see your friend? I'll let Doctor Sidhu know you're here."

As soon as he entered Wheat's room, Simon sensed something was different. He crossed the room in a hurry, afraid of what he'd find. Wheat was no longer stretched out on his back, the covers neatly tucked under his chin. Instead, he lay on his side, one arm draped outside the covers.

Simon hadn't realized he'd been holding his breath until it escaped in a whoosh. He took the old man's hand, intending to put the arm back under the blanket. The arm jerked. Simon's gaze flicked to Wheat's face. Confused eyes looked back, then cleared.

"Simon?" The word was more croak that speech.

Simon poured a glass of water, found a bent straw and held the glass for the old man to drink. When Wheat pushed the glass away, Simon pulled up a chair.

"We were beginning to think you planned to sleep the rest of your life away."

"What happened?" Wheat asked.

"Don't you remember?"

Wheat's gazed flicked around the room and he groaned. He struggled to turn on his back. "Put this damned bed up so I can see something."

Simon complied and waited for Wheat to settle himself. He asked, "What do you remember?"

"Hoisting a few at some bar in Coos Bay. Where am I? How'd I get here?"

"You're in the hospital in Lion Rock. You had an accident."

"Was I drunk?"

"The doctor says no. I think you were run off the road."

"My truck?" When Simon hesitated, Wheat said, "Oh, shit. Everything gone?"

"Almost. I salvaged a few things. Can you remember anything about the accident?"

Wheat stared at the ceiling, his face screwed into a frown. "There was a big black car. That's all I remember."

"What about before the accident?"

"Oh, shit. I guess I'm in real trouble."

Simon waited.

Wheat cast a quick glance at Simon, then looked away. His fingers played with the sheet.

Finally he spoke. "I swiped a few of them leaves. This guy

up in Coos Bay buys them from me. Done it a couple of times before and nobody seemed to notice. Didn't figure they'd miss just a few leaves."

"But this time they did notice?"

Wheat shrugged. "I don't know. But this guy kept buying me drinks and asking where I got them leaves."

"Did you tell him?"

"I don't think so. I don't know. Maybe. I was pretty drunk."

"But you weren't drunk the next morning."

"Nah. I slept it off in the truck."

"This bar where you met your buyer. Did you recognize anyone from Lion Rock?"

"Wasn't looking. 'Sides, the place was packed. Could have been, I suppose. You reckon that's why they run me off the road? 'Cause I'd been swiping their leaves?"

"Maybe, but I don't think you have to worry about them anymore."

Simon stayed until the doctor came and assured him that Wheat was on the mend and any danger was past. He'd be able to leave the hospital in another couple of days.

Simon stopped in the hospital lobby and used the pay phone to called Lovey and report on Wheat. His stomach grumbled as he left the hospital. He realized he'd had nothing to eat since breakfast that morning.

He drove to the Seaside, expecting Ruthie to be ready to close. The place was packed. He leaned against the wall, waiting for a seat, and listened to snippets of the excited conversations going on around him.

"...Tredmore blew a gasket when all them cops showed up..."

"...I hear they had to carry him out..."

"...biting and frothing at the mouth..."

"...Who'd have believed..."

"...found all kinds of drugs in that warehouse..."

"...on his boat..."

"Hey, look. Cass Owens has got them two toughs of Avery's! Busted them all, by God!"

Simon glanced out the window and watched the cruiser

drive toward the jail.

At last the crowd thinned and Simon took a seat at the counter. Wearing a tired smile, Ruthie took his order. He ate while she cleared the tables. When the last customer left, she flipped the closed sign on the door, poured herself a cup of coffee and took a seat beside Simon.

"Busy night," Simon said as she lit a cigarette.

"Yeah. Most excitement this town has seen in donkey years."

"Just came from the hospital. Wheat regained consciousness and is on the mend. Doctor said he could leave the hospital in a few days."

Ruthie's face lit up. "So that old fart's gonna make it. I'll go by and see him tomorrow."

"I think he'd like that."

Ruthie gave him an intent look. "You're gonna be leaving."

Simon nodded. "In a couple of days."

"You have anything to do with all this mess?"

Simon raised an eyebrow. "I don't know what you mean."

Ruthie chuckled. "This was a nice, quiet little town 'til you came. Now all hell's broke loose."

Simon shrugged and ate his dinner.

THE NEXT morning, he checked out of the motel. Back on the mountain, he found everyone gathered around the fire ring. Andy was there, although there was no sign of his gear.

George waved him over. "Grab a seat. We're just deciding on what's best to do."

Billy Joe said, "I got a gig tomorrow night at the LOG JAM." George looked at Simon and asked, "Can you give us a ride to town this afternoon to pick up our truck?"

"Sure. Why don't we all go in and visit Wheat?"

Meg shook her head. "Jamie and I will stay here, but you tell him we're thinking of him."

Lovey rode with Billy Joe. George and Frannie asked to be dropped off at the garage. "We'll come by the hospital as soon as we're finished here."

Simon led the way to Wheat's room, but stopped in the

doorway. Ruthie was seated beside the bed, Wheat's hand clasped in both of hers as they gazed into each other's eyes. Lovey shoved past Simon, breaking the spell.

"This old fart's gonna come and stay with me for a while," Ruthie said. Wheat just grinned.

George and Frannie arrived and they all visited until it became obvious that Wheat was becoming very tired. As Simon was leaving, Wheat called to him. "I remembered. It was kids. They was racing." Wheat grinned and winked. "Leastways that's what I told the police this morning."

Simon returned the grin and flipped a salute as he walked out.

Back in camp, they gathered around the fire pit. George broke the silence. "Tomorrow's the Fourth of July. You're staying for the celebration, aren't you, Simon?"

Simon hesitated.

Lovey gave him an intent look. "Sure he is."

Simon shrugged. "Why not. We'll all be there. Meg, don't you think Jamie would enjoy the fair?"

Lovey said, "Of course she would. Be good for her to be around people again."

Meg shook her head. "I just want to go home."

Simon hesitated, then said, "I'll be heading north myself. If you want, Meg, we can convoy as far as Portland. In case you have car trouble or something."

He glanced at Lovey. "What are you going to do?"

"Oh, I think I'll just stay right here until fall or until they run me off. Then I'll head down to Arizona for the winter. Andy'll help me when I'm ready to go."

George said, "I guess Frannie and me'll head out with Billy Joe for California."

THE NEXT DAY, Simon helped the others load up for the fair and watched as Billy Joe and Frannie and George pulled out. Although Lovey's car and trailer were still parked, the little clearing that had been his home for the last months suddenly seemed empty and forlorn. With a sigh, he waved goodbye to Lovey and Andy and drove slowly out of the clearing, following

Meg's station wagon.

It had been an interesting few months. He'd made new friends and he'd miss them. He consoled himself with the thought that his great adventure had really just begun. There was still a lot of new country to see and new people to meet.

After crossing the Columbia River, Simon picked up the cell phone and dialed his son's number, but only got the answering machine.

"Orin, it's Dad. Just crossed the Columbia and I'll see you tonight."

The End

Judith R. Parker

Judith R. Parker is a former teacher and corporate CFO. She is the author of several award-winning novels and numerous short stories. Before turning to fiction, she wrote for professional journals on "boring subjects such as accounting procedures."

She currently makes her home in the Cascade Mountains of central Washington State with her husband, two dogs and six cats.